Housewife! I hear you say. Has Jonny been having one of those peculiar operations? Surely he values his credentials too much for that!

But here he is at Withering Bumple, in the home of the lovely Lobelia Dugfondle, an ex-actress who never forgets her loins; who is willing to forget about the rent in return for . . .

When the merry widow wins a holiday competition for spotting the ball (!) Jonny finds himself holding the fort (amongst other things). And looking after Lobelia's seventeen-year-old daughter, Charity. Even with the threat of the blunt scissors hanging over his, er, head, can Jonny resist her ample charms?

Read on and all will be revealed. Several times . . .

Also in the 'Confessions' Series and available from Sphere Books

CONFESSIONS OF A WINDOW CLEANER
CONFESSIONS OF A DRIVING INSTRUCTOR
CONFESSIONS FROM A HOLIDAY CAMP
CONFESSIONS FROM A HOTEL
CONFESSIONS OF A TRAVELLING SALESMAN
CONFESSIONS OF A FILM EXTRA
CONFESSIONS FROM THE CLINK
CONFESSIONS OF A PRIVATE SOLDIER
CONFESSIONS OF A SHOP ASSISTANT
CONFESSIONS OF A TRAVEL COURIER
CONFESSIONS FROM THE BEAT
CONFESSIONS OF A GAMES MASTER
CONFESSIONS FROM A STRIP CLUB

Confessions of a Housewife

JONATHAN MAY

SPHERE BOOKS LIMITED
30/32 Gray's Inn Road, London WC1X 8JL

First published in Great Britain by Sphere Books Ltd 1976

Apart from the numbers of kind friends
listed in the next four pages, this is also
for Guy Smith. With every good wish.

Set in Intertype Lectura

Printed in Great Britain by
Hazell Watson & Viney Ltd
Aylesbury, Bucks

DEDICATIONS

My Publisher tells me to keep it shorter, but that's obviously only a bit of jealousy on his part. But here we go with the names – and other things – of all of you who've written in to me at my Publisher's in the last few months. Isn't it exciting, seeing your own name? For those of you who missed this deadline and who've written in, or are still thinking about writing in, there will be more of my adventures coming along, so be of good heart. And read inside details of how to do it . . . not 'it' . . . I mean 'it'.

So here we go . . .

First a couple of specials. And nobody's more special than Ann Summers of Aylesbury. Last time I spelled her name wrong, so this time I'm making sure it's right. Ann Summers. With lots of thanks for everything.

Janet Collins of Chard for the Christmas card and for the photo. Thanks.

Rosemarie and Kim Gee from Guildford in New South Wales. Beautiful pictures that cheer me up on cold days.

There'll be one or two other special mentions to come, so keep looking.

One last special. Rob Edwards from Dulwich. A great bloke. And if anyone's interested in buying a juke-box, then give Rob a ring. His number's 01-670 6935. Seriously.

Lilian Parton from Walsall – so near to my old home – and Reg and Martin and Jimmy and Frank and Arthur and Tony and all the gang in the games room at Beechdale Social Club. And a right lot they sound!

Janet Royston of Westcliff-on-Sea.

Irene Inkersole, David Baylis and Lesley Baylis, who are also from Westcliff-on-Sea.

Glynis Kemp and Sue who are both twenty-six. Well, they were when they wrote in. And they're from Sittingbourne.

Robert Wiggins (Worzel) and Sambo, Melon, Kev, Mott, Ian and Wayne.

Helen Lester, Karen, Harvey and any fans. From Stafford.

Duke and Blue for the card. They also get a mention in the book, the lucky people. For those who still can't work it out, my birthday is 24th September, and I'm Libra. So now no one has any excuses!

Mrs. Kathleen Greaves of Ward End, Brum.

Dora Ellen Rowland – the sexy redhead at the dry-cleaners. That's what she asked me to put. Honest!

P. D. Gardner from Leeds. And for him and lots of others, I am not Timothy Lea and I am not Rosie Dixon nor am I Oliver Grape. Not now and not ever.

Linda Alexander, Vici MacDonald, Maureen Scoble and Christine Walker. And they also want me to mention Gary Glitter. All right – Gary Glitter. Satisfied?

To Mike from Guy (I told you I would). Actually, I don't know what it means either, but that's what this bloke from Bristol asked me to put.

Mandy and Debbie who are both pretty and slim, but they chickened out of sending me their address, or their photos or any frillies. Despite all that, they still get a mention.

Roger and Jayne. Thanks for the card.

Margo Anderson from Glasgow. Thanks for the folding card. As I pulled it out it got bigger and bigger, and that can't be bad.

Roland Dunn (thanks for the jokes) and his friends Rayce Staples, Bill Bailey, Steve Hussey, Gal Lambert, Brian Togwell, Yvonne Sissons, Timmo Rudling, Rachel, Lynn, Karen, Leslie and Sticky. Don't anybody blame me if any names are spelled wrong. Some of your writing . . . !

Elaine Byrom from Batley. Thanks for the brow-wipers. They're starting to get worn out now, so anytime you've got more . . .

Gary Ursin-Smith from Shrewsbury.

Arnold Kitching, Marion Quickmire and Shildon Town C.C.

Kathy Withington from Wigan, who sent me a really smashing letter. Shows that flattery gets you anywhere.

Mrs. Puttock of Nottingham and her son in the force.

Bill Kirby of Enfield.

Dave Batten and Dave Weeks both from Ludgershall in Wiltshire.

Colin Banks, his wife Maureen and the Engineers at Palmers Green Telephone Exchange.

Linda Fennell and Simon Barnett who is gone but not forgotten. From Brentwood. Hope you still remember him, Linda.

Ricky (The Big Yin) and Marie and the families about to be united by matrimony. I don't know what a Yin is, but I hope it's not rude.

Valerie Barnes and Jill Riches. Vivienne Barnes, Paul Barnes, Deirdre Barnes and Mum and Dad Barnes. From Harrow.

Fiona Taylor and Keith Lightbown. From Nuneaton.

Frances Smith, Steve Smith, Peter Cooper and David Driver, from near Chelmsford.

Terry Stevens from Cardiff, who on his own admission must now be the happiest sod that side of the Severn Bridge.

Ronald Carey (Atom) and Katie. From Maerdy.

The Eastleigh, Hants, Branch of the J. May fan club. That's Derek Tomlinson, Terrina Stamp, Brian Towers, Mandy Mole and Stephen Folliot.

Steve Furnish from Basildon.

Joan Dunglinson from Walsall, with all best wishes.

Jim Salkeld and Corinne Britten. Hope the wedding went well.

Derek George Woollard Marsden, from Chelmsford. And that's all one name.

Gary Anthony Smith and Stanley Bertram Smith, who's his old man, from Aberystwyth.

Juliana di Claudio – what a lovely name – from Calne.

Susan Heritier and her husband Jean-François from Lausanne.

Kay Quilkey and her brother-in-law, Brian Newcombe. From Australia.

And this is for Amanda Keown, who is chasing Wayne, but he stops too often. That's what Amanda, from Palmerston North, New Zealand, wanted. And thanks for her thanks note.

Ron and Lee Holt from Western Australia.

Bronsonlane from Western Australia as well, and they know who they are.

Trudy Garrett from Dunedin in New Zealand.

John Ferguson from Bondi in New South Wales and the boys from the Mansions Hotel, Kings Cross.

John Davies and Santiago and everyone who works in the Britannia Restaurant on the QE2.

Barbara Lock and Sandra Carter from Auckland, New Zealand.

Mr. P. Perkin from Crediton.

Taffy and Jenny Raybould and Junior (hope it arrived safely) and Private Alan Christmas (my Publisher wouldn't let me use your nick-name). And the Ystradgynlais All Souls Social Club and Institute.

D. C. Jupp of Worthing. His is the shortest – dedication, of course.

Mrs. Alma Clarke and Mrs. Carol Weaver from New South Wales.

Marilyn Martin of P.O. Box 6305, Wellesley Street, Auckland, New Zealand, who is 22, unmarried, and likes netball and watching rugby. She'd like a penfriend, so get on with it fellows.

Now for John Hunt and he wants a book to himself. I just hope all this lot each buy a copy of the book otherwise I'll sue them for sore typing fingers. This is worse than Two-Way Family Favourites. Terry Jones, Andrew Vincent (alias Dick Withers!), Howard Freemantle, Mick, John and Dennis Coates, John Sutton, John Campbell, Pete Campbell, Rob Harrison, Tony Hiser, Steve and Kev Harris, Pete Aries, John and Sarah, Eggy (Big and Little), Andy Rogers, Kip, Wonk, Woody, Spray, Sammy, My Mum – I mean John Hunt's Mum – Blimey, leaves you a bit late on his list, doesn't he? Patti, unless he means that's his Mum's name. Step-father Jazz, big sis Sandra and her husband Dave, his nieces Sarah and Vicki, little sis Becky, Nan and Pop and Lin and Steve. He hasn't finished yet the cheeky . . . ! The ship's company of H.M.S. *Mohawk*!!

A. R. Webber of Coventry.

Nick Sullivan and his mates Ray, Dave and Bill. From Croydon. John D. Knowles, and Keith Burgess, Stephen O'Garra, Paul Ingham, Stewart Parker, Arthur Buck and Paul Kelly (who is a copper, but we won't hold it against him. After all, he wouldn't hold it against us.)

Sex-mad Martin Pemberton of Blackpool. And, ugh, the things I do to keep a promise, he asks me for a dedication to . . . I can't do it. Not Chelsea Football Club. All right then. Chelsea.

Terry Green, George Crow, Richard Mulley, Bernadette Rooney,

Lorraine Byrne, Celestine Foran and Roma Campbell, all from Peckham, and you see where your threats of violence have got you.

Trevor Bennett from Australia.

Diane Heath from London makes it two books running for a lovely letter and a special present of *two* pairs of frillies. What a wonderful example. Thanks for the supports and I wear them constantly!!

Susan Parry, who is an Elvis Presley fan. And so is anyone with any sense, including me. So there!

Jock Dunlop, Roy Thornton and Slim Cordingly from the Ordnance Depot in Antwerp.

Dirty Dave from Derby. No comment.

Mike Orford, Jenny, Joe, Arnie, John and M.M.

Janet Mather and Susan Bimpson from Leigh.

Someone else coming in for two in a row and bonus points. David Ward and the Barbra Streisand Association. And he also wants a dedication for Dot, Karla ('I shan't') Spooner and Anne ('Don't feed the kids') McLaren.

Paul Hayes of the 1st R.H.A.

Karen Staples wrote to tell me that she'd got married since her dedication in 'Strip Club', and she wants a word for her new husband Ricky Staples. Congratulations to both of you and a big thanks for the big frillies.

Bill Wright, his wife Frances and his daughter Linzi.

Jack Cross and the movers at Brize and also Pat Salmon and Nicky from London.

Doug Wells, from Nelson, New Zealand.

Carol Everitt from Wolverhampton and her friend, Reg. One day I might take her up on one of her nice offers.

All New Zealanders and particularly John Newport (who wrote the letter), Karen Osbourne and Karen Smith.

Bernadette Jones, her husband and her two and a half kids. I hope by now it's at least three. She's from Western Australia.

Tony and Sheila Hughes from Rumney and their friends (and/or relations) Gordon and Lorraine Hughes and Fred and Edith Probert.

Gerard Baynham of Penarth.

Keith Williams once of King Edwards, Birmingham. Wonder what happened to him?

Cherry and Tracey, the two flying posties from New Zealand.

Rosemary Sellan (I think that's it) from Grove Park.

Richard Handscomb, all the way from Oman.

Sandra McGregor, Sonia Key, Fred McGregor and Denis Key, from Auckland in New Zealand.

Bob and Jane Greening from Southsea.

Philip Terry, Winfield Vaughan (known as 'Big Frank' for what Philip says are obvious reasons) and Brian Miller. They'd all like to be . . . Sorry, the Publisher won't let me tell you. You'll just have to guess.

Linda Westwater from Bermuda. If I'm ever out that way, I'll look up you. I mean look you up.

Barbara Scott, Barbara McLennon, Barbara Gott, Barbara Lochie, Christine Schum, Yvonne Baxter, Annette Nyland and Debbie McGuinness. I expect a package of eight pair of frillies from you lot!

Richard William Mortimore from Bourne End.

Andrew Bale who is yet another from the dedications pages of 'Strip Club'. This time he also wants a mention for Sue Cox. So he gets one.

Ken Longley from Staines.

Nick Rogers from Scarborough, and Bob, Ginny, Fuzz and Oxfam.

Miss Lesley Hayes, who sent me a particularly nice letter from Invercargill in New Zealand.

Taff O'Mahoney, Gordon (Scotty) Mackay, Lloyd (Bullet) Adams and Paddy (Brummie) Banks from 44 (Rhodesia) Squadron, RAF Waddington, Lincoln.

Graham Bowers from the Isle of Wight.

Jan Mingins and Doreen Goss from New Zealand, who were nearly but not quite too late.

Donald, Jim and Avril, Dave, Susan, Wee Katrina, John, and Helen from Hinckley. Not forgetting Kenny and Stuart from Torrance.

Elizabeth Howells, Mark Howells (hope you're now allowed to read my masterpieces), Graham Carter and Denise Paul (who ought to buy her own copies!)

Ann-Marie Dodds from Andover and her brother in the Metropolitan Police.

Geff and Joyce from Gwent who sent me a lot of jokes and a thing fourteen inches long. It was a letter on a big piece of paper!

Liz Wheadon who used to live in Handsworth Wood. Wonder what happened to her?

Ruth Logan who comes from Londonderry but is at the Loughborough University of Technology. At least she was when she wrote.

Christine Jones and the Pine End Works in Lydney.

Nick, Bundy, Sue, Allan, Jane, Ken, Shirley, Martin and Sue all from Stroud in Gloucestershire who use the most amazing notepaper you've never seen.

Two to go.

Rol, Steve (Short ***), Staples (Ears), Bill (Stub-eye), Tim (Dainty Crutch), Brian (who throws money about like a bloke with no arms), Nick (the Chelsea Yob), Dave (Speakeasy), Benny (from Benidorm), Sticky (The Fish) and Garry (Spotty) who all come from Enfield and support Tottenham Hotspur Football Club. Oh, well! Better than Chelsea, I suppose. And thanks lads for a great lot of jokes.

Last one just before the deadline for this book is a lovely one to finish on. Actually, I'd rather start on her. It's Pandora, who you've probably seen in the audience at wrestling matches on the box. She's called 'The Duchess'. Lovely pair of frillies she sent. Matched my eyes. Sort of pink.

And on her behalf, for Mick McManus, Harvey Smith, Steve Viedor, Wayne Bridges, Ivan Penzekoff and Spencer Churchill.

That's it. The rest of you who've written or who are writing will just have to wait until the next stupendous volume of my memoirs.

Keep the jokes and letters and frillies coming in. And a big thanks to all of you.

Jonny May, February, 1976.

CHAPTER ONE

Hello.

My Uncle Angus goes to this big wedding a year or so back. Keeps his drinking to its usual moderate level, which is half a centimetre below the top of his throat. Note that this is the first metric 'Confessions' book. He eats a vast meal, with three helpings of prawn cocktail, nine chicken legs and eleven bowls of trifle. Starts feeling a bit less than well, so he goes off into the library of the house. Uncle Angus sits down on the sofa, feeling a rainbow belch on the way. Up it comes. Unnoticed by Uncle Angus, the hostess's cat has walked in and is sitting by his feet as he throws up.

All over it.

Uncle Angus glances down at the mess on the floor, where there is this puke-covered pussy. Staggers to his feet, saying: 'Blurry 'ell! I don't remember eating that!'

That's just to give you the flavour of the book, in case you'd forgotten.

(Publisher's Note: As if I could enjoy such good fortune. It's all on account of Mister May that my wife says I wake screaming in the middle of the night.)

If I had his wife then I'd wake screaming in the middle of the night too.

Enough of this light-hearted banter. Not 'batter', missus. That's something old and greasy that pads out your . . . on the other hand. . .

A little later I shall bring you tidings of comfort and joy, and I'm not talking about new detergents, of special interest to those who think they know a lot of jokes. But more of that later.

Now, on with the story.

I said: 'Now on with the story!'

Oh, well, but I had been promised a fanfare of trumpets. All I got was some Fine Fare crumpets.

Anyway, on with the story.

Early morning. Dull, misty, grey morning. Cold as a witch's . . . culvert. Quiet side street in a small village about twenty miles north of London. Not far from the place where Jonny bared his all in a bare hall in *Confessions from a Strip Club*. Place called Withering Bumple. Honest! I don't make all this up, you know.

One or two happy commuters trudging down to the station to catch the seven thirty-five to Liverpool Street. Well, it's generally the seven forty-something. If it comes at all.

But hark! That means listen. There is the merry jingling of milk-bottles further down the lane. I really think I'd better not tell you the name of the little road, because you just won't believe it, and that wonderful trust between me and you will have been broken faster than my old man's wind.

If you promise to believe. Makes me feel like Tinker Bell asking if you believe in fairies. I do. Remember Rupert Colt from *Confessions of a Travel Courier*? If you ever meet Rupert then you'll believe in fairies as well.

The lane is called Copper Bottom. Since I'm plugging all of my other books, I should say that is Copper as in Beeches and not as in *Confessions from the Beat*. I miss the police force in some ways. The truncheon vouchers came in handy.

The jingling gets nearer, and we can hear the cheerful whistling of the person in the white overall driving the little truck. Merry little trucker!

It stops outside number eighty-four. A smart pair of black

shoes come tramping up the neat path, bordered with as fine an assortment of weeds as ever graced 'Bill and Ben'. Three pints of gold-top chink on the doorstep. Actually, I can't stand this Chinese milk. Rat-a-tat-tat goes the lion's-head door knocker. As nice a knocker as I have seen since Lop-Sided Louella chose the balcony of the Beacon Cinema, Great Barr to join Women's Lib and get rid of her bra. Turned into an enormous flop though.

Rat-a-tat-tat. What a load of tats! There is the noise from within of someone shuffling along in down-at-heel slippers, and the clatter of bolts and chains. Alongside the milk-bottles, the black shoe taps impatiently. What can this deliverer of pintas be waiting for?

I know you think you can guess! And I can tell you that you are wrong.

Wait and see.

Just as the hand goes up to the knocker again, the door edges open. The whistling stops, and a big smile breaks across the face of the above-mentioned milk-deliverer. Talking about whistling, I suppose you know why Brummies whistle when they're having a pony and trap on the toilet? You don't? It's so that they can remember which end to wipe!

'Hello,' says the face behind the door.

'Hello, darling,' replies the face outside on the step. Those morning steps can be very chilly. Worse than the Russian steppes in fact. 'Got time for a quick cup of coffee for me?'

'Course I do. Come on in. I've got the kettle on ready for you.'

The milk truck stands solitarily at the side of the lane while curtains twitch in neighbours' windows. The front door shuts.

We are now inside the house. Number eighty-four Copper Bottom. And it is very crowded with all of us in there! Actually, there is just one man and one woman in there.

As well as . . . 'Keep quiet. The kids are still asleep and I don't want them waking up.'

Two pairs of feet tiptoe up the stairs, and along the landing. One pair is in bedroom slippers, and the other pair are naked. The black shoes are in the kitchen, under the table. A bedroom door swings silently open, and the two people go in. And that door also closes.

All along Copper Bottom, folks are having to wait for the milk for their morning cuppa. And all through Withering Bumple as well. My brother Morrie, who you will recall having tripped over in other of my adventures, was once a milkman. He reckoned his slogan was 'Laya Housawife A Day'.

And I am beginning to see what he means.

A pair of blue pyjamas and a brown dressing-gown bite the carpet, followed in no time at all by a pair of dark blue trousers and an overall. Off with the underclothes in no time flat. That's the trouble with doing a milk-round *and* doing a bit of over-and-under-time as well. It has to be a bit of a quickie.

But that's better than no quickie at all.

I shall now pass further along the book and avoid all those boring descriptions of naughtiness that have ruined earlier tales of handsome Jonny May's adventures. A lot of you have written in to me after my promise to mention you in dedications (see the front of this book and you'll find I keep all of my promises) and you all said how the naughty bits put you off reading.

Believe that, folks, and you'll believe anything.

Some of those letters were amazing, and if I took all of the ladies' invitations up, I'd be worn to a thread.

(Publisher's Note: Such modesty.)

He can talk. His is worn to a thread before he even starts!

I was also delighted to see how many of you young ladies followed up on my suggestion and sent me your old frillies to wipe away the sweat from my brow. My brow is now free of sweat and my old man is peddling the frillies in West Bromwich market. But keep them coming ladies.

Now, hands up all those who want to read about what seems

likely to happen between this housewife and the mysterious person in the overall and the gold-top. Who can he be? I hear you whispering.

Hands up. Did I tell you about the bank-robber who gets up late, parks the getaway car on a double yellow line, drops his mask, falls over the steps of the bank, goes up to a closed counter and snarls: 'This is a cock-up!'

All these hands going up. And all those dirty minds licking their lips. Right then. If Mrs Mary Whatshername would like to put this copy back on the shelves, I'll get on with it.

If I remember rightly, we had two members of the opposite . . . gender; I refuse to use the word 'sex' in any of . . . I suppose I have. Opposite sex, neither of them with any clothes on, in this bedroom, early in the morning. That's mainly for those of you who start reading a book halfway through the first chapter. If you have, then you've missed an amazing anecdote about the Prime Minister of a major European country, a famous pop star, a camel and a dustbin full of luke-warm custard.

Incidentally, if you cross a camel with a ghost you get things that go hump in the night.

The lady lies back on the bed, and Jonny lets his hands roam freely about her hills and valleys. There is no doubt about me getting a welcome in her hillsides. Edgar is perking up. In fact the very first rat, not to mention the tat-a-tat, on the knocker gets him raising his head.

We lie together on the soft double-bed, and she gets her fingers to work with the marriage equipment, though marriage is still many a long mile away from my mind. My right hand drifts down her body with all the grace of Charlie George slipping round a defender and nestles into the warmth between her thighs.

Whenever I see a button, I just have to press it, and in this case the response is very satisfying. For both of us. She moans like the lonesome whistle of the San Francisco Flyer taking a crossing in the middle of the night. I *don't* know personally, but I've seen it on the telly.

I am glad that I've trimmed my fingernails, and wince slightly as Edgar discovers that the lady hasn't. But he's past caring by now. Her chesty regions make an ideal home for my left hand which also loves to go a'wandering. I use my index finger to run rings round her, and that nobbly bit in the middle promptly rises to the occasion faster than one of Fanny Craddock's little cup-cakes. And if you haven't nibbled on a little cup-cake then you haven't lived.

The lady gets her morning tit-bit, and I slide down and give a demonstration of what a cunning linguist I am. I am not going to tell you the lady's name, although she is on the tip of my tongue.

After he lost all of his teeth, my Uncle Angus used to reckon that he was one of the best at that sort of oral examination. Claimed he could suck the middle out of a grapefruit at ten paces. And spit out all the pips.

Either there is an earthquake hitting Copper Bottom, or the lady is beginning to rise and fall like a line of washing in a force nine gale. Trouble is, every time she brings her hips up, my nose gets banged. Comes of putting my nose into other people's business. I have to say that before my publisher sticks his in.

From this position, the only comfort that Edgar gets is by being sandwiched between the lady's feet, which are fortunately very soft. Comfort is two things called softness!

But Edgar would rather be taken in hand than in feet, and I remove my mouth from that creamy little honey-pot, and begin to slide up again, faster than the Financial Times Ordinary Share Index. Whatever that is.

The lady is thrashing around, and I fear to let her get her hands on Edgar. She reminds me of a girl I used to go out with in Birmingham, who worked nights as a lady wrestler.

After a session with her Edgar used to come out looking like a pound and a half of best mince.

By cunning use of my knees, I manage to slide the good ship Edgar into port – and starboard as well – where the lady is so glad to have him aboard she grabs me round the neck and buries her tongue somewhere near my left tonsil. Once aboard the bawd I grab hold of anything I can and hang on, feeling like a bronco-buster. But where would I get one at that time in the morning?

The bed has some of those carved wooden balls at the end, and I manage to brace my feet against them for a bit of leverage. I can push going in, and hook my toes round them on the way out. You know the sort of carved wooden balls I mean, don't you missus? The sort you park your chewing-gum on for the night. Nothing worse than picking a bit of dried gum off the balls in the morning, that's what I always say.

Her thighs are up round my waist, and I can feel her ankles locking behind my back, sort of drawing me deeper and deeper into her. I am boldly going where no man has been before.

Actually, I don't reckon that's true; not the way she's built. Reminds me of the time my bike broke down in the Mersey Tunnel. In fact, the very first time that the delivery of milk at eighty-four coincides with a bit of the other, I ask her during a rare quiet moment if I'm the first man she ever had it away with. She looks at me and shakes her head. 'I don't think so, although your face is familiar.'

By Pin and Ball! Things are rising and falling faster than the Third Reich. My veal vibrator is rocking and rolling like Chuck Berry with the wind behind him. A momentary worry crosses my mind about the noise waking the children, but their bedrooms are on the other side of the house, so I continue to plough the field, and soon reach the moment where I am about to scatter my good seed on the land. Not really; not on the land. More, sort of up a leafy lane.

Edgar gets put under all sorts of pressure, which leads me

to the conclusion that the lady is ready to end this particular indoor game. In fact she goes directly to 'Come', and there is barely time for me to spur Edgar on to collect his two hundred pounds at the same time. As I have remarked before, it is not polite to go through a door before a lady, so to speak. On the other hand, it is a bit of a drag to find yourself left outside after she's finished. If possible, I always try to squeeze through at the same moment.

Just like in books.

'Thanks, Jonny love,' she says, giving me a nice sloppy kiss on the cheek.

I kiss her back. Well, I've already kissed her front, haven't I? She gives me a hug and a squeeze, and Edgar starts to wonder whether things are going to end up in some extra time. But the lure of the gold-tops must come first, and there are the children's breakfasts to cook. So I give her a last friendly pat on the bottom, and we both slide squelchily out of bed.

Know what I mean?

My Aunt Holly, who is a prickly sort of a person, and who has recently got married to a new uncle you haven't met before, called Old Uncle Nick – or Old Nick for short – is a right little goer. I'm never sure of her exact relationship to me, but we have had our ups and downs, and I shall say no more. It was thinking about that pleasantly sticky feeling that somehow made me think of her. She is once asked to address the local Women's Institute on the subject of 'Personal Marital Relationships'.

She stands up and looks at the audience, still sweating from the eighteenth chorus of *Jerusalem* and says: 'Personal marital relations. It gives me great pleasure...'

And she sits down again.

Having mentioned Uncle Nick, I suppose I ought to give you a quickie so that you know the sort of thing that runs in the family. Like wooden legs. I'm not saying that our family is particularly stupid, not by Birmingham standards, but it gives you an idea of things when they call me the Bertrand Russell of the May family. And it's not just because I've got long hair.

Uncle Nick walks around with his flies undone in case he has to count to eleven in a hurry!

I help the lovely lady on with her flimsy tight black lacy knickers, pulling them carefully up over her long firm thighs, and pressing them into her pussy pelmet so that they nestle snugly in place. There! I hope you enjoyed that bit as much as I did.

Actually, I really like helping girls to get undressed. It's better when they *want* to, but it's fun anyway. And it's not bad helping them get dressed as well. Although it's sad bidding a fond farewell as the land of nookie vanishes slowly in the gusset.

Never mind . . . see it again, another day, like they say in those kids' books about the old man with the boat and car. I used to read them to the brats of a neighbour in Great Barr to get them to sleep. Not like Jonny May, you might say, and probably will. But if you'd seen the neighbour, you'd know why I was in such a hurry to get her kids off to dreamland so that her and me could follow their example.

Her knickers are on. I peep through the curtains, and it's getting lighter, though the weather looks about as inviting as a goal-less draw between Spurs and Arsenal on a wet Saturday in November.

'Time to be getting on,' I say.

'Yes, love. Time to be getting on,' she replies, joining me at the window.

'Same time tomorrow?' I ask.

'Yes, love. Same time tomorrow.'

While she stands next to me, peering through a crack in the curtains, her left hand starts off again, raising Edgar to unexpected heights. I stop peering through the curtains – hope the printer doesn't leave the 'r' out of that – and make a grab at her, but she has moved back and is finishing putting on her clothes.

'Sorry, love. But I've got to go and get on with things now.'

'Wouldn't mind getting on with your thing,' I reply, with all that famous May charm gleaming out through the pearly-whites at her.

'Now, now,' she says.

'Now! Now!' I shout, diving across the bedroom at her, but I catch my toe in the edge of the carpet and bark my shins, and bite the rug to stop screaming aloud. The bark is much worse than the bite.

The agony eases, and I stand up.

'Bye love,' she says, kissing me on the cheek.

'Bye love,' I reply.

And *she* goes out and carries on delivering the milk while *I* go and make the breakfast for the kids.

Bet you can't wait to find out all about it, can you?

CHAPTER TWO

A HOUSEWIFE! ! !

I can hear the screaming from here, drifting in above the thunderous noise of an aeroplane roaring in to land. It is called a 'Whisperjet' I notice.

Yes, a housewife. That's what it says on the front of the book, and that's what it's all about.

Has Jonny been having one of those peculiar operations? No, he hasn't. My credentials are far too valuable for that sort of thing. Some men might fancy getting cut off in their prime, but I am not one of them.

So, what can it all mean? As the stripper said: 'All will be revealed.' Talking of strippers, my Uncle Nick once fancied having a go at being a male stripper, but he suffered from clothestrophobia. I'm not saying that Uncle Nick hasn't got the same kind of brain as Uncle Angus, but someone asked him if he knew what claustrophobia was, and he replied that it was a morbid fear of Father Christmas.

No dear, I'm not going to explain it. Ask the man in the next seat. He's doing what? Well, that's fairly common. He's what? Oh, using your hand to do it with! !

Let's get back to the main issues. I like those man-sized issues. The wet-strength ones. What is Jonny doing getting laid by the milk-delivering lady on a cold morning at eighty-four Copper Bottom, Withering Bumple?

Well may you ask. Well may you ask May. May you well ask May, may you not.

I shall have to recap a bit, like cuddly Lady Isabel used to mutter on *What's My Line*. This is also another excuse to plug all the other books in my adventures.

All my loyal and devoted readers of previous adventures can

go and make a cup of coffee for the next paragraph or so while I explain about my past to those stunningly lucky people who are here for the first time. And we all know that everyone always remembers the first time.

When I first come down to London from Birmingham, a year or so back, I work in Stoppers of Knightsbridge, which is a store so exclusive that even the mice have credit accounts. My adventures there are recounted in *Confessions of a Shop Assistant*. Then I have a gay time working for, but definitely not under, Rupert Colt in his holiday emporium. In *Confessions of a Travel Courier*.

I feel a few collars, among other things, in *Confessions from the Beat*, and then have many ups and downs in an amazing educational establishment for young ladies. This leads to *Confessions of a Games Master*.

Notice that my publisher never interrupts me during these commercial breaks. I'd like to break his . . . but let it pass.

But thinking of game reminds me of the time my Uncle Angus went hunting. Sees this naked lady lying spread out in the middle of the wood. Looks down at her over the barrel of his twelve-bore and says: 'Are you game?'

'I am,' the lady replies.

So he shoots her.

At this point you have to follow closely. Not that closely, you'll get us both arrested. Before I am a Games Master, I work in a Strip Club, in a variety of unusual positions. But before I write *Confessions from a Strip Club*, I write the Games Master book. Right? And please don't ask why, because I can't remember.

So. If we slip back in time to the end of July, we'll find ourselves at the end of Games Master.

Incidentally, I'm asked by my publisher to point out to you that all the above-mentioned rib-ticklers are available from Sphere Books at ridiculously low prices. Ask at any book shop or newsagent.

I get a card from my brother Morrie after the school job comes to a climax that makes *Towering Earthquake Disaster '77* look like *Stars on Sunday*. My brother Morrie, short for 'Morello' which is my mum's favourite jam, is the potato on the exhaust-pipe of life.

Like another man I know who is also in publishing, Morrie's motto is 'Anything you can do, I can do later'. I've never met such a crooked bloke. I'm not saying that every part of him is twisted, but he once chucks this girl he's going out with, muttering something about her having a left-hand thread.

He'll do anything for money. He once meets this amazing old scrubber at a dance, and he takes her along to a theatrical agent he knows. Walks in and says: 'I've got this woman outside on the landing. Wait till you see her. She's got the most fantastic figure. It's 99–28–60.'

'Ninety-nine! Twenty-eight!! Sixty!!!' screams the agent, nearly swallowing his cigar.

'That's right.'

'Stupendous!! What can she do?'

Morrie shuffles his feet. 'Wellllll. With a bit of help she can sit up.'

This card brings a mixture of emotions to my mind. Like watching your mother-in-law drive over a high cliff – in your new car. It says: 'Dear Jonny, If you are looking for a job, I can find you an interesting position with lots of openings. Love Morrie.'

Lots of openings!

Could be very interesting.

That's what I think. But I also know my dear brother, and I have my suspicions.

However, with nowhere to live, and with no job, I would even leap at the chance to march on parade behind the Royal

Canadian Mounted Police. It would be a big opportunity to really clean up.

So I ring up my dear brother, catching him in his office. When he answers he says: 'Chinese Takee Outee. Hao Hi speaking.'

'Hello Morrie,' I say. 'Honestly . . . Hao Hi, indeed!'

'About five foot eight actually, if you must know. Good to hear from you Jonny. You got my card?'

Knowing him, I'm surprised it wasn't the ace of spades. Though he never calls a spade a spade.

'Before I forget . . . Melanie sends her love.'

Melanie is Morrie's twin sister. Being sent love by her is something like the black spot. In 'Treasure Island', missus. Not a nasty pimple.

Now I won't say that Melanie is a revolting and amoral little nymphomaniac with anti-social habits and some unpleasant friends.

On second thoughts; that's such a good description of her that I *will* say it. I'll give you an idea of what she's like. After getting kicked out of a lot of schools, mum and dad send her to a very strict convent way out in the country. Two days later she's back. Expelled for doing press-ups in the cucumber patch.

'What's the job, Morrie? The one with lots of openings. I could do with a spot of the ready.'

Or ready-or-not here I come. My wallet is flatter than one of my mum's sponge cakes. They're the only sponge cakes I've ever seen that you could actually use to wash with.

He looks sheepish. Since he normally looks foxy, Regent's Park Zoo would probably be interested in him.

Morrie shrugs his shoulder like he's auditioning for Shylock. 'Jonny, my dear brother, it's like this . . .'

I will cut a long and tortuous story short to please you and my publisher. The job with lots of openings is doorman at a hotel run by a friend of Morrie. If you knew Morrie like I know Morrie, Oh, Oh, Oh what a ****. The word doorman should equal bouncer. The word hotel should equal one of those establishments with a red light over the door and rooms you book by the minute. They have rooms in all sorts of colour schemes, but the most common are the tartan rooms.

(Publisher's Note: I personally found this alleged 'joke' quite incomprehensible, until my secretary – a nice enough girl I always thought – explained that it was a play on words. It meant 'tart an' room'. Tart and room. I thanked the girl for her explanation and took the next opportunity to sack her.)

Lucky girl, say I. Working for him must be like getting hit on the head by three hundredweight of noisy pink cement. Pink because it suits his complexion.

So much for Morrie's openings. We exchange a few pleasantries, and he tries to borrow a fiver off me, which is like trying to win a heckling competition with Harold Wilson. He's known as Doctor Heckle and Mister Jibe.

So I'm on the streets. You are wondering how the homeless and unemployed and penniless Jonny May is miraculously transformed into a housewife.

Patience.

And while you're at that, try the red queen on the black king.

I leave Morrie's temporary office, where he is talking about setting up a special hospital for people with chronic constipation. But with friends like Morrie, who needs enemas?

It's raining.

All of my stuff is parked with various ladies here and there around London. But I fear that I would not be welcome with any of them. There was also a card waiting for me from a lady who has appeared in other of my adventures. The lovely and clever Elizabeth James.

She and I have had our ups and downs, not to mention our ins and outs, but she is always moving on, while I am always standing still. Last I heard she was touring America with a long-haired poet who was into certain intoxicating substances that I have only heard of. He was always rolling stoned, so she said.

The card said the poet had run off with a twenty-five stone black lady called Beulah and Liz was on her way home. I thought it might be worth going and looking up her . . . I mean looking her up, at the flat she keeps in Notting Hill.

Despite the rain making my collar wetter than a balcony seat at a Bay City Rollers concert, the thought of Liz makes the sun shine.

I fumble in my pocket finding, in order, a grey handkerchief, sixty-eight pence, a hole and a cheap thrill. I withdraw from the pocket billiard championship and decide to risk it all on a cab.

There is a taxi unloading on the other side of the street, and I run for it with all the lithe grace of an unleashed panther.

(Publisher's Note: Ruptured penguin!)

Talking of lithe grace . . . lovely lady she was, amazing grace we called her back in Great Barr because of this trick she had of whistling up . . . I was talking about athletic skill.

It runs in our family. Uncle Angus decides he'll have a go as a professional boxer and models himself on Muhammad Ali. With typical Uncle Angus cunning he goes into his first fight and floats like a bee and stings like a butterfly.

My Uncle Nick's not much better. The one who's married to Aunt Holly. The origin of her name is deeply berried. He thought he'd go one better than Evel Knievel. So he drives a truck right over fifteen motor-cycles!

Remember it's raining, and as winter draws on . . . I've had mine on for weeks . . . the street is darker than a camel's coal-hole. I arrive at the door, pull it open, and leap in. The next thing I know is that I have caught my stacked-heel boots in my flared turn-ups (I always had a flare for turn-ups) and I dive into the back with all the charm of pert little Olga Korbut.

Which would be fine if there wasn't already someone in the back of the taxi.

I expect to find my nose buried in the dusty old upholstery of the cab. Instead I find my nose buried firmly between a pair of firm thighs. Which fit me perfectly, as I try them on for thighs. If the truth is to be told, my nose isn't actually between the legs of this unknown lady. It is just a little bit higher. Sort of . . . how shall I put it?

(Publisher's Note: Careful, Mister May, or we shall all end up in the Old Bailey.)

For those of you who know, then no explanation is necessary. For those of you who don't, then I'm afraid you'll just have to wait till you're a bit older.

Although my ears are compressed tighter than sardines in a tin, I can just hear a muffled squeak. Sort of squeaklet. I reach up to try and free my head, and find myself in even deeper waters.

Good job I don't suffer from water on the brain. As I carefully slide my hands up between the lady's legs, my first thought is that she must be a nun, wearing those hairy knickers as a penance. Did you know that nuns advertise for penance-friends?

But it is not a nun wearing very hairy bloomers.

It is a lovely lady wearing no bloomers at all!

I blush deeper than a gay spider caught with a claw in someone else's flies.

The cab-driver is nearly suffering a rupture of his neck trying to twist round and see what's going on in the back of his hansom. His mouth sags open like my old gran when she drops off in front of the telly watching the eighth repeat of *The Forsyte Saga*. I have the foresight to miss it.

I kneel up, conscious that the unaccustomed proximity to the naughty parts of a member of the opposite sex has roused

Edgar to new heights, making my Oxfam trousers strain at the tapes.

'I didn't know you were engaged,' I stammer to the lady, sitting back on the seat, adjusting her clothes in a white froth of undergarments. Petticoats and all that. There is also a fair flashing of leg.

'I'm not engaged, my dear young man. I was married, but I have since broken free from that dreary trap.'

Nice voice. Like honey poured over port-coloured velvet. Sort of nicely aged and smoky. Like Fenella Fielding. That sort of voice.

I'm still on my knees, and the driver now seems to have decided that nothing too violent is going to happen in his cab.

' 'Ere! The lady was 'ere first, so you better scarper out of it.'

He has a point, but I don't like his manner, and I am prepared to offer him that famous old Birmingham delicacy, a knuckle sandwich, when the lady interrupts.

'Since I'm in no hurry, I can wait and you may drive this young man to his destination, and then carry on to mine.'

The driver grunts and grumbles like an elderly steam engine, but finally turns round and slams the cab in gear. The back door is still open, and I'm nearly thrown out, but I manage to save myself and sit on the seat, calling out where I want to go.

After that, there's a breathing-space for me to sit back and look at my saviour. I can still savour her too.

I suss out fast that she is unlikely to see her thirtieth birthday again. In fact, I'd be surprised to learn that she is the right side of forty. But she is better preserved than most of my mum's jam. I'm not saying that it used to go off fast, but my old man never used to take any bait with him when he went fishing in the cut. Just a pound jar of 'Blackberry 1956'.

The lady wears a black fur hat, perched on blonde hair that I guess owes a fair bit to the hairdresser. A brown suede coat, over dark stockings, and I know that they aren't tights. Not unless she's got *enormous* holes in them. And brown suede boots.

From what I remember, she is wearing a grey woollen dress underneath the coat, and layers of lace. And underneath that? Sweet nothings.

And very sweet nothings they seemed to me on my brief acquaintance. Not that she has any briefs to acquaint myself with.

She spots me giving her the eye and grins at me.

'Nicest introduction I've had in a long time, sonny. Suppose we ought to at least say who we are. My name's Lobelia Dugfondle.'

With a name like that, it's on the cards we might get to be bosom friends. There is still that delicious hint of passion-pit lingering on my lips as I grin back at her.

'I'm May.'

'And so may I dear, but let's get the names over first, shall we?'

'No. I'm May. That's my name. Jonny May.'

What I don't understand is that my publisher tells me that thousands of you read my books, and one or two of you actually buy them first. So there must be a lot of people around who know that when I'm asked my name, I reply 'I'm May'. But I still get the same old joke. And I believe in passing everything on.

(Publisher's Note: The only thing that Mister May ever passed on to me was a nasty case of flu one Christmas.)

I want it known that the very same Christmas he's moaning about, he gave me an even nastier case of cheap Beaujolais.

Lobelia smiles at me like a cat who's got the cream, and we knew what Jonny thinks about a contented pussy. 'Jonny. That's a nice name.' The traffic is fouled up like a saucepan of cold spaghetti, and we are making less progress than a ruptured snail. 'Looks like we're going to have a bit of time together. Tell me a little about yourself, Jonny.'

She leans back and crosses her legs, showing a vast acreage of creamy, firm, rounded, kissable . . . Sorry. I also cross my legs in a vain attempt (I'm so vain) to hide Edgar rising to the occasion.

As we crawl across London – still in the taxi, you silly person! – I tell Lobelia about my life. I leave out one or two bits. But it still comes out sounding like a male version of the *Jolly Fisher*. Sorry; I mean the *Happy Hooker*.

She nods her head and 'Ooohs' and 'Aaaahs' in the right places, digging me now and again with her elbow at some naughty part. I think I prefer her 'Aaaahs' to her elbow.

It cannot be concealed that Jonny is down on his luck. If I saw a black cat it would probably just walk over and pee up my leg. I tell her where I am going and why, and I notice that she is beginning to get 'that look' in her eyes.

As we near the last known address of the lovely Liz, the traffic thickens again, so Lobelia edges nearer to me across the dusty back seat and tells me a little of her life. She is coy about her age, but reveals that she has three children, the oldest of whom (grammar) is seventeen. She is a widow, her late husband, Reginald Dugfondle, being a successful plumber who finally went right round the S-bend and ended his days making baskets in the Sunnydale Farm for Distressed Artisans.

Lobelia was also something on the stage, and I am not talking about the 3-10 at Yuma. Feeling her hand doing a slow foxy-trot up my strides, I can also believe that she was something behind the stage. She hasn't played any parts for some years now. But she is doing well enough playing with mine. I thank the personal gods of the May family that the taxi-drivers in London aren't allowed to have mirrors that show them what's going on in the back of their cabs.

I gather she never made it to the top. 'Not like you, Jonny. The way you dived in on top of me, you started with the bottom.' She giggles in a not unpleasing manner.

I also gather that her favourite topic is covered in rich

chocolate and . . . Whoops. I meant that other topic. Where was I? Gathering. She is gathering in the darling nuts of May, and seems prepared to sample them right away. They are the sweet things you can nibble on between meals and not lose your appetite.

What I was trying to say before I interrupted myself was that Lobelia likes to talk about herself. I have never known a taxi ride take so long yet pass so quickly. Lobelia is a fund of the most amazing stories about people in the theatre. Famous actors and actresses that you see every day on telly and in films.

They are so incredible that I've decided to devote the next dozen or so pages to just a few of them. They'll make the *Sun* look like the back page of the *Financial Times*.

Here we go.

(Publisher's Note: No we don't. It cost us a lot of money paying for our lawyer to recover in hospital after he read the first page of Mister May's stories. His last words, whispered from his bed, were: 'I'm not saying that they're libellous, but if you go ahead I hope you book your ticket to Rio first.' If I tell you that the mildest of them concerns a well-known and much-loved actor from a telly series, eight schoolgirls, a railway compartment, a pair of sweaty socks and a plate of hamburgers! ! Need I say more?)

Yes, he need. He could have mentioned the mustard. That's the point of the story. Still, if he's going to be a party-pooper and spoil things, there's not much I can do. But it really is a shame. You'd have loved the one about the ferret and the commercial for soap powder.

From what I can hear through the muffled grunts, it seems that Lobelia has been left well-provided for, and lives comfortably in a cottage in a village the name of which I don't quite catch, but sounds like Smothering Pimple. But it's hard to tell as Lobelia believes in talking with her mouth full. A fact that neither Edgar nor I find at all offensive.

'What number, Guv?' coughs the driver, fortunately without looking round.

'Sixty-nine,' I squeak back. Sitting back. Holding back. Helping Lobelia to a more dignified position on the seat beside me.

'So near and yet so far, Jonny,' smiles the lady. 'You've no idea how much pleasure that gives me.'

I do have an idea, as I have been able to use my early training as a contortionist to get my ten little soldiers marching bravely up her mountain. When they march into her valley they find that it has turned into a soggy swamp. Not an unpleasant feeling at all.

I reckon the driver must have had lessons from my old man, as the cab stops dead in its own length, throwing us around like a couple of dried peas on a shovel. I mutter another prayer of thanks that Lobelia wasn't deep-throating me at the time, or she might have done me grievous bodily harm.

I don't, incidentally, want to give you the idea that my old man is a bad driver. He is a *rotten* driver. He got really well-known around Great Barr for it. I remember he once crashes head-on into the vicar's car. Out gets the Reverend Makepeace, shaking like a leaf in a thunderstorm. Out gets my old man smelling like a brewery at full production.

The vicar waves away my old man's mumbled apologies. 'Please, Mister May. I beg you not to reproach yourself.'

'I don't your reverence,' belches mein papa. 'It makes you grow hairs in the palm of your hand.'

'Tut, tut, tut,' goes the Reverend Makepeace, sounding like an Egyptian archaeologist with a stammer, 'I mean that the accident was entirely my fault.' Since my old man swerved clean across the road and hit him coming out of a drive, I am impressed with the logic of this.

'Indeed, Mister May,' goes on the sky-pilot, 'I saw you coming for at least three hundred yards and there was ample time for me to have driven up a tree.'

Lobelia kisses me hard on the mouth, and I find that the tip of my tongue has somehow crept in between her lips and my hand is wandering away again up happy valley. There is a cough like a bronchial seal-lion from the front of the cab, and we part rather reluctantly, with a noise like pulling the cork out of a bottle of homemade wine.

'Remember, Jonny. If your friend isn't able to take you in, then I'm sure I could use an extra pair of hands about the house.' I'm sure she could. 'And the children do sometimes run a little wild.'

That doesn't sound so much fun. But she is a well-matured hunk of meat is Mrs Dugfondle, and I am a great believer in the idea that there is no substitute for experience. Some of my happiest times, and Edgar's too, have been with ladies old enough to be my . . . well, older sister, let's say. Not only are older ladies very good at it, but they are also very grateful.

'Thanks a lot, Lobelia, That was a trip I'll never forget. Can I contribute to the cost of the taxi?'

By the Buddy and the Holly! As I get out I notice the amount showing on the meter. I have not been in a cab for some time, and the price has rocketed. At first I wonder whether the cost is, in fact, the price that he is selling the taxi for, but I quickly realise it isn't. I suppose it's all the fault of metrification. Changing the meters.

'No, no, no, dahrling,' she calls through the open window.

She does pronounce it like that. 'Dahrling.' A hang-over from her actress days, I suppose. But I am grateful to her for refusing my aid. Because I had less than enough aid and that would have made me feel a right lemon. Sort of lemon-aid, if you know what I mean.

As I walk up the path towards number sixty-nine, I notice that she is keeping the cabbie waiting. I've heard about golden minutes, but to keep a taxi waiting like that must mean golden seconds. Her late husband must have left her very well-off indeed. Obviously a shrewd business-man. Not like my Uncle Angus who once broke into a betting-shop and lost five pounds.

Lobelia's other source of income is competitions. You know the sort of thing. Identify these famous ears and write us a free advertising slogan and you win a week in Llandudno. Second prize a fortnight in Llandudno.

The good folks of Llandudno will probably be steaming at the navel at such a slight on their town. 'Why us?' I hear them cry. The answer is that I once sent back one of those furthest-distance balloons to a competition in Llandudno, and I reckon I should have won a prize, because it was about two hundred miles. Never even got a reply! So, after all these years, I take my chance to pay them back.

Like elephants, we Mays have long memories.

Which reminds me of a question that my young sister Melanie once asked me, which struck me as not unfunny: Do you know why elephants have big ears?

You have to say: 'No.'

Louder.

That's better.

The reason that elephants have big ears is that Noddy wouldn't pay the ransom.

Boo-boom.

Well it's better than the one about what goes 'Ha, ha, ha, ha, ha, clunk?'

Give up?

A man laughing his head off.

Lobelia has told me that in the last five years since she started doing these competitions seriously, she's won two cars, five freezers, nine holidays and enough food and drink to keep the house going for years.

'But I've never had any luck spotting balls,' she tells me.

She could have fooled me.

Number sixty-nine is a huge Victorian pile in the middle of Notting Hill. With all those Victorian piles, I'm not surprised she wasn't amused.

There are those tiny mail-boxes by the door, and one of them has the name of Elizabeth James neatly lettered on it. It's open, and I reach inside. There is a note inside.

Equally neatly lettered.

Dated today's date. Timed just over an hour earlier.

'Dearest Jonny. If you're reading this, then you must have come round after all. If you're not, then whoever is reading it must be the new occupant of the flat. Hope you enjoy living here more than me. But if it's still Jonny, then I'm ever so sorry, love, but I didn't hear from you, and I couldn't seem to catch up with you. I had a chance this morning to go up to Edinburgh and work with that new Italian film director, Luigi Lusta, you know. Had to make a quick decision. Sorry we couldn't get together. If you want to, leave me an address here and I'll pick it up one day. Lots of love. Liz.'

I find that I've got something in my eye, and blow my nose hard to clear it. Maybe one day. Maybe.

A voice from the street changes my mood.

'Jonny! Bad news?'

I walk slowly back to the taxi, where Mrs Dugfondle is looking worriedly out of the window at me. I crumple the note up and stick it in the pocket of my jeans jacket.

'Yeah. She moved out this morning. Gone up to Scotland for a time.'

'Scotland! I once did a commercial up there for fish-fingers. All oilskins and wellies. Horrible place. Full of hairy knees and stags at bay.'

I stand there looking at her, feeling like a spare alcoholic at a temperance wedding. On the debit side Lobelia looks as though she might be one of those possessive birds that want to have Edgar in their hand as well as in their bush. And she is no Spring chicken. More of an Autumn broody hen. But, as my close examination of her more private assets revealed, she is in good shape.

Which is more than can be said for my assets.

Not Edgar, though he could do with a bit of fresh-air after being tripped up just short of the finishing-line.

I mean the possessions of one Jonathan May, bachelor, of any parish you like.

They are scattered all over London. The only things that I have in any one place are my threads and my sounds. The former are mainly blue denim, as this is hard-wearing *and* I just like them.

Regular readers will have some idea of my likings as far as sounds go. John Stewart and Doctor Hook. Beatles and Buddy Holly. Sha Na Na and Elton John. New Riders and Eagles.

There. That should keep me in freebies for a few months. Come on you record companies!

Added to that are all of my other possessions.

Like. . .

Not to mention. . .

As well as. . .

And there's. . .

By Bank and Ruptcy! Things are not well with Jonny.

(Publisher's Note: We've known that for a very considerable length of time.)

I shall ignore that withering shaft of wit. Or was it a waft of ****?

All right, officer. I admit it. I'm broke. Got nowhere to live. And no job. So anything is better than nothing.

'Why not come and live with me for a bit, dahrling? Help out around the house?'

If this is the fate worse than death that my old mum was always warning Melanie about, then I'll take it. Melanie's been taking it for years and it doesn't seem to have harmed her.

I remember that when she was fifteen, mum sends her to a Sunday School to try and improve her mind. First time there the vicar – it was old Reverend Makepeace, I believe – was giving a sermon. At least, I think it was Makepeace, but the church of Saint Arbuthnot Atte Barre changed vicars so often we used to count the number of revs per year.

Anyway, his sermon is about how it is possible to conceive as a virgin without sinning. Up goes Melanie's hand. 'Please sir. I'm much more interested in how to sin without conceiving.'

The first few days pass in a haze of beds and food. My duties helping out Lobelia at eighty-four, Copper Bottom, Withering Bumple are minimal. Though Lobelia constantly tells me that Edgar is one of the least minimal she has ever seen, and I soon know that I am in the hands of an expert.

Her children seem to accept me with a quiet mixture of loathing and hatred, regarding me as the pips in the grapefruit of life. But more of them in the next chapter.

Lobelia is not joking when she says she's well-off. I bet you've never seen a mink jacket?

On the lavatory seat?

But she still has this thing about competitions. Gets every paper from the local shop, and all the magazines and food packs with quizzes or anything on. I reckon she must spend about fifty quid a week on these things. She buys two hundred of Chunkodry – the new food for doggies, made from recycled goats, just for the labels. Arrange these five well-known footballers in alphabetical order and say in not more than twenty words why you think Chunkodry is the best food for your pet.

Trouble is the only pet Lobelia's got is a toothless budgie. And he is bound to succeed.

I shall now sit here and wait until the rest of you get that last joke.

Succeed.

Toothless budgie.

Succeed.

Say it out loud. Succeed.

Oh! I can't wait any longer.

Suck seed!

The competition that she most wants to win is one she has been doing for weeks on the packet of Sunnycrud. The breakfast cereal that comes ready digested. What you have to do is complete five well-known sayings. Sort of things that test even the brain-power of the average Brummie. Like: 'Cool as a—'. To make it easier they give you three possibilities. For that one they're these: 'Cucumber'. 'Microphone'. 'Mole'.

Pretty tricksy, you must admit.

After you've struggled with that, then you have to make up a slogan for Sunnycrud. Lobelia comes up with: 'Start the day the proper way – with Sunnycrud.'

I reckon her chances of winning are twofold. Infinitesmal and nil.

But the prize is certainly worth having. Six weeks holiday for one in sunny Crud. Sorry, in sunny Barbados, with all expenses paid. I think it was Barbados. But I know it's in the West Indies. I tell her if she wins I'll look after the house. I only say this so that I can tell people that Mrs Dugfondle's gone to the West Indies. And they'll say 'Jamaica?' and I'll say: 'No, she went of her own accord,' and I'll burst out laughing.

Actually, I do say it to her, but she doesn't smile. Not a great sense of humour, Lobelia. But she really reckons she has a chance and thanks me for my offer of running the house in her six week absence. As though yours very truly could possibly run a house for six minutes. Especially with those three demons of kids to look after.

The very idea makes me shudder.

Hey, you. The blonde one giggling in the typing pool there. I'm sure you're very clever to see what's coming, but don't spoil it for the others. And stop giggling so much. If you go on like that you'll wet. . . Have you? Well, that just proves that I'm right, doesn't it?

I remember the morning it happens. When I die, they'll open me up and they'll find the word 'Sunnycrud' engraved on my heart.

Lobelia and I are in bed, where we spend much of our time. I have promised to go off to the nearest town to do a bit of shopping for her. She wants some paté. My old man's got a bald pate, I tell her, but she doesn't care.

I am sealed up in her jamjar, with the old veal velocipede doing its stuff. I have one hand on her left hillock, while the actions of the other make me feel a right tit. She is panting and moaning like my publisher when he has to write a cheque. Her fingernails are turning my shoulders into Ordnance Survey maps of Snowdonia. There's no Donia like Snowdonia, is what I always say.

There is a ring on the bell.

'Postman!' she shouts, blowing on my drum. Ear-drum, love.

The bell rings again.

'I'm coming!' she screeches, rushing away from me, leaving Edgar wondering who turned on the light.

'So was I,' I protest feebly, but it's too late. I can't even be bothered to shake hands with the country's future.

There is a muffled noise from downstairs, like the lid blowing off a pressure cooker, and then an ominous silence. I get up carefully, wondering if the bomb has landed and I'm the only survivor. The kids are all at school, so we have the house to ourselves.

Lobelia is standing at the bottom of the stairs, looking up at me with an odd expression on her face. She's holding a letter in her hand.

'Jonny, dahrling?'

'Yes, dear.' She likes to be called 'dear'. For this sort of life I would be prepared to call her Adolf Hitler.

'I . . . I wonder when you're going down to the shops for me.'

By Hitch and Cock! Twenty-eight seconds ago we were busy

stoking each other's fires. Now she just wants to rake over a few ashes.

'I'm going when I'm dressed. I'll be about an hour and a half.'

There is that odd expression again. 'All right dahrling. You are a sweet boy, Jonny. And I trust you with everything. You do mean all the nice things you say, don't you my dear dahrling?'

'Why, of course.' I am wondering what I might have murmured in an odd moment, and I do have some very odd moments.

'Splendid. I am sorry about leaving you up in the air, so to speak. Now hurry on down and get me some more of that Plymouth Tea.'

Plymouth Tea!! At least I think that's what it's called. A name that sounds like that. I cannot understand why she wants to have that stuff. I really can't. I prefer Edmond's Home Brew, myself, but there's no accounting for taste.

I shall now cut a longish story very short. I leave the house with a farewell kiss like the end scene of *Queen Christina*. Anyone would think she wasn't going to see me for years.

I do the shopping and come back round about mid-day.

There is a white note pinned to the front door.

I read it.

The next-door neighbour, the nosy Mrs. Vatman, who is a taxing sort of person, sees me looking like I've just met a ghost. I admit my thunder has been struck.

'What's wrong, dear?'

I wave the note like it's peace in our time. 'She's gone and left me. Gone to the West Indies.'

'Jamaica?'

'No. She went of her own accord.'

And I burst into tears.

CHAPTER THREE

I don't really burst into tears.

Not quite.

Nearly. But not quite.

Although I am far from in the mood for humour, my publisher insists that I put a joke at the beginning of each chapter. Not that he understands half of them.

Well. Here's a quickie about my dear old Uncle Angus.

Despite all his faults, it has to be admitted that he was somewhat generously endowed in a certain area of his body. No, I won't spell it out. But you know that you get a little prick if you catch your little finger on a little thorn on a little rose on a little bush?

Uncle Angus has a big bush with big roses and big thorns and he also has big fingers. I shall say no more.

But he decides to go to this Fancy Dress Ball (?) dressed as Adam. Calls in a theatrical costumier and they send him a fig-leaf.

He tries it on and it's much too small. Rings them and tells them, and they send him the next size up.

Still a lot too small.

Rings them up to complain, and they post him the largest fig-leaf they've got.

He opens the package, rushes upstairs and tries it on.

Goes down to the phone and calls them up. 'Sorry to have to tell you that this last fig-leaf you sent me is still a lot too small for me.'

There's a long pause the other end of the line, and finally a weary voice comes on. 'I think that we can solve your problem for you, sir.'

'Tell me, tell me,' bellows Uncle Angus.

'Stuff it in your ear and go as a petrol pump!'

Back to the front door-step of eighty-four, Copper Bottom, Withering Bumple, where the skies have just collapsed on yours truly. I feel lower than a beetle's bazooka.

Mrs. Vatman is still lurking on her doorstep, trying to look inconspicuous. She is about as inconspicuous as a kangaroo in a cocktail dress. I manage a smile and walk quickly through the door of eighty-four.

I get up, rub my nose and try it again, this time remembering to open the door first. I close the door and go into the living-room and sit down on an over-stuffed pouffé, and no jokes about that please.

The note is still in my hand, and I smooth it out and lay it on the table with all the grace and care of Hudson serving the morning sherry in the Bellamy household.

There are marks that indicate it has been written in haste, leaving me time to repent at my leisure. The blue felt-tip pen has been used that Lobelia normally employs to write her shopping-lists and milk orders.

'Dear Jonny,' the note begins, 'Dear Jonny, this will come as a bit of a shock, darling.' She spells it like that, even though she says it 'dahrling'. And she can say that again about it being a shock.

I remember one Christmas Eve back in Great Barr when I've had a drop too much of Gran's elderberry wine and stagger off to the crapper feeling in need of a quiet sit-down. I've hardly got my strides round my ankles when there's this noise like a bomb going off, and something wet and furry strikes me from beneath. Right up the Khyber. I leap from the seat faster than my old man out of a pub when his round comes around.

I am out of the door before you could shout 'Bullocks!' up a long entry. Into the hallway, with my trousers still nestling about my ankles. Thank the stars, there is nobody out there, as I present an embarrassing spectacle. Even a pair of spectacles.

Edgar is in such a state of shock that he has retreated without leaving a trace.

For a moment I think of that awful bit in *Jaws*, when the naked bird who's just had it away, finally has it off by the shark. Perhaps the monster, whatever it was, has severed my pride and joy, and I'm numb with shock. Fingers trembling, I have a quick grope around underneath, and am more than a little relieved to discover that all is still there, though hardly in fighting condition yet.

The blood of the Mays is roused. And when that happens we can show all of the raw blood-and-bones courage and tenacity of an earwig with its back to the wall. Though it may cost me dear, I go back in the bog to face this lurking creature from the primaeval ooze. This blasphemous entity from beyond space and time. This nameless . . . I must stop reading all that H.P. Sauce Lovecraft stuff.

Grabbing a handy length of four by two left over from my old man's last flirtation with the DIY bug, I walk boldly back in the toilet.

And peer bravely into the bowl.

Empty.

By Chuck, Elder and Berry!! That wine was strong stuff. I am about to drop the chunk of wood and resume my normal activities, when there is an explosion of water from within the toilet and a rat bursts out like a Polaris missile. With that greased perfection that made me such a foe to be feared on the rhubarb-thrashing courts of Europe, I catch the bleeder a swift one round the ears, and flush it away out of sight, never to be seen again.

Honest. I swear that this is a true story. So are all of them, but this one is *even* truer than others.

Well, those of you with memories that go back two pages, you might recall that I tell you this story to point out the degree of shock I have just got from Lobelia's note. And to compete with a wet rat snapping at your short and curlies, then it's got to be really something.

It is.

It goes on: 'I was as surprised as you when the mailman brought me a letter today from the Sunnycrud people. Saying that my entry had been the best they'd seen.'

I have to admit that I am rather impressed with her entry as well. And her exit isn't bad.

'The only thing is that I have to go straight away to start my prize. The letter had been delayed by the Post Office.'

Well, what a surprise! A letter delayed by the Post Office! Whatever next I wonder. The twenty-five pence one-class delivery, guaranteed delivered within six months. It used to be faster in Africa when they used a big bloke carrying the mail in a forked stick.

'I have to be in the airport by lunch-time, and we will be in the West Indies tomorrow. See you in six weeks. Lots of love, Jonny, and thanks so much for offering to run the house for me while I'm away. I'll make it up to you when I get back. Fondest kisses all over dear little...'

There it gets all a bit personal. Lobelia is a great one for pet names. Having it away with her is like a walk through a child's garden of whimsy.

Blimey! Not that snobby detective, Lord Peter Whimsy!

There is a P.S.

'I will write you while on the train to the airport to give more details of what needs to be done about the house.'

And there is a P.P.S.

'But while I remember. Make sure that C. gets her knickers off every night.'

I will.

Believe me, I will.

Which makes it as good a time as any to tell you all about Lobelia Dugfondle's little brood.

Charity is the eldest. The 'C' that Lobelia refers to. And the mention of her knickers is to remind me of her strange habit of keeping them on all night. Says it saves her getting cold. From what I have seen of sweet Charity, I would be surprised if it ever had time to get cold. She makes my sister Melanie look like the Mother Superior of a closed order of nuns.

I'll give you a couple of examples of the sort of behaviour I mean. There is a programme on politics on the box, and I ask Charity how she's going to vote. She looks blankly at me and says: 'Quite honestly, Jonny, I just don't care who gets in,' and she winks.

Lobelia wouldn't believe it, of course. And reckons that the sun shines out of Charity's. . . I reckon that many a son has been shining out of Charity's . . . but Mrs. May's wee boy Jonathan is not among them. More than my life would be worth if Lobelia caught me up to it. And anyway, I'm not sure that I am up to it. Not with seventeen year olds any more.

But Charity begins at home and carries on anywhere she can. If she ever gets, by what would have to be a miracle, to Heaven, she'll be straight up to the Celestial Quarter-master's Stores. To swap her harp for an upright organ!

There are two other members of the coven. Or do I mean family? I see that a coven is a group of like-minded wicked people united in evil purpose. That's as fair a description of the Dugfondles as I could think up.

Faith is twelve. A twin with the face of Twiggy and the soul of Norman Hunter. She has a twin brother. Which completes the trinity. Faith and Charity and Robert, known as Bob.

Bob as in Hope, you see.

Faith, Hope and Charity, I abide with these three, and it's hard to tell which is the worst.

And for the next six weeks I shall be acting as father to them and as a housewife to eighty-four, Copper Bottom, Withering Bumple.

There's only one word for it.

Aaaaaaaaaaaaaaaaaaarrrrrrrrrggggggggghhhhhhhhhh!

I should like to seize this opportunity to thank all of you who've written in to have your name in the dedications. By the time this epic appears it will be too late for any more of those, though I may possibly reopen the idea again at a later date. What I'm going to do this time, with the cheerful and willing co-operation of my publisher, is to have a competition.

You have to keep on reading this rib-tickling, side-splitting extravaganza to find out the vital details of what to do. When to do it. And how to do it. All that information, you lucky folks. All I'll tell you at the moment is that it is not totally unconnected with jokes, and that there will be a handsome prize.

(Publisher's Note: I suppose he means me.)

Handsome!! Him? The only time that's true is when he hands some money over. He's the only bloke I know who keeps the milk money in an un-numbered deposit box in Zurich.

I'm not saying he's mean, but he's the only person I know who took his iced lolly stick back and asked for a discount because he'd read the joke on it. His idea of a three-course meal is fish, chips and peas.

But, all of this notwithstanding (and notwithsitting either) he has still agreed that some sort of prize will be given for the best joke or jokes sent in. He hasn't said how much yet, but if you keep on reading, then by the end of the book I hope he'll have told me and I'll tell you. So don't send any jokes in yet.

Wait till you reach the end and then you can. If you've still got the strength.

I'm not saying that ladies who send in frillies with their entry will have a better chance, but I am going to be one of the judges. Nudge, nudge . . . know what I mean.

I was going to go on and tell you about my first evening as a housewife, but I reckon it's time we had a break. And a Kit-Kat. So here's a quickie question for you.

If a light sleeper can sleep with a light-on: Can a hard sleeper sleep with . . . a window open?

CHAPTER FOUR

Since that last chapter ended on a low tale, let's begin this one with a high tale. It's another question, and it's not about the giraffe being the only animal in the jungle that can walk into a cocktail bar and say: 'The highballs are on me.'

No, it's not about that.

Do you know what the difference is between an Opera Director and a baby?

You have to say: 'No. What is the difference between an Opera Director and a baby?'

And I say, with a knowing leer and a nudge in the ribs: 'Well, the baby is the one who sucks his fingers.'

And then you laugh.

Gawd! Forget it love. If the penny hasn't dropped by now it probably means the lock's faulty.

I sit in the living-room for nearly an hour, trying to take stock of the situation. It is clear that Jonny is out on his own this time. Nobody to share the problem. So the stock has no shares.

The house isn't that big. Four bedrooms. Garden of about half an acre. Not too much to do there at this time of year. Bit of digging and rooting around. Burying my implement in the fertile soil. Sort of thing I'm good at.

In some ways this might be quite a challenge. I've always had this theory that women are rotten at doing women's work. Know what I mean? They have eight cups of coffee with their mates from next door, vacuum the floor, wash a couple of pairs of socks, and unfreeze a packet of fish fingers. That's what they all call a hard day.

My old mum used to be like that. And that sort of hard day was her excuse for not having it off with my old man. That or a headache. Then again, if you knew my old man you might reckon that she has good taste. The best she could hope for was to lie back, close her eyes and think of England.

But I mustn't malign my old man. Remember that old TV game, *What's Malign?* He isn't that bad. I remember the romantic evenings they used to have together. With dad's head resting gently on her shoulder.

I used to carry his feet.

Now's my chance to prove my theory. I know that Lobelia's left plenty of bread in the musical cigarette box on the sideboard. The one that has the little Dutch boy on the lid who raises his hat and pulls out his black pudding when the music plays. And knowing her, she'll have made some kind of arrangement for money while she's away.

I'll also prove another theory. Women are lousy shoppers. Spend far too much on rubbish that the supermarkets palm off on them under the disguise of special offers. They won't catch me like that. I don't like those places anyway.

It's a vault! It's an aircraft hangar! It's a SUPERmarket!! I don't see anything super about them. I shall probably do my shopping during the next six weeks at the little old corner shop. Just like my little old mum did before me.

That is, if I can find one.

As you may gather, May is beginning to look forward to the idea. It'll be like a six weeks holiday. With pay. What I'll save from the housekeeping. Pleasant house to live in. The last couple of years have hardly been notable for their peace and quiet.

There will be a shortage of nooky, but I can put up with that if I have to. And from what I recall of my last experience of the young ladies of Hertfordshire villages (See *Confessions From A Strip Club*) there might well be a few local lovelies eager to let me hang my bed-socks on their lines.

I believe I shall be blessing the name of Sunnycrud over the next few weeks. The thought pleases me so much that I rise and open the Dugfondle bar, disguised as a row of plaster ducks flying across a mirror, and take out a bottle of best Polish vodka. One hundred and forty proof. Lobelia has introduced me to it, and we get on rather well. Like a house on fire, in fact.

Come to think of it, the effect is rather like being in a house on fire. The moment it hits your mouth it feels numb, then your breath goes. Shock sets in, and there's a burning sensation in the throat. After a minute or so you can breathe reasonably freely again.

After one you feel that you could tackle the world. After two you feel you could tackle the universe. After three you couldn't give a monkey's about anything. After four you fall asleep.

I'm not saying how many I have, but I find that I can think better about the problems facing me if I close my eyes.

Just for a moment.

After all, there's nearly three hours before Faith and Robert are let out.

Ho, hum. Merriment and what-not.

Golden slumbers kiss my... !

'Blurry 'ell. Look what the blurry cat's dragged in and left on the floor!'

Can it be the dustmen?

No, it's the son of the family. All twelve years of him, back from his seat of learning. And that is where I would like to boot him. Right up his seat of learning.

Robert Dugfondle, who shall hereinafter be called 'Bobby' as the party of the first part. He stands about the average height for a depraved twelve year old. In some books you might read of such characters who have the faces of angels and the manners of fiends. Not Robert. He has the face of a demon and the manners of a demon. So I suppose you could say that he had the virtue of consistency.

I wake up. I mean I stop thinking with my eyes shut and

look blearily at him. 'What are you doing home from school so early, my little one?' I ask him.

He looks at me like I'm something he's just scraped from the bottom of his football boots. Not that Bobby ever involves himself in such healthy pursuits. Smoking and gambling, and other vices I'd rather not mention are more his sort of pursuit.

'Wodgermean? Not blurry early. Normal blurry time you stupid git! Where's me blurry tea and where's that old bag sodded off to?'

Now I give you my word, and Jonny's word is his bond, as you know, that it has been my intention to be calm and sweet and reasonable with little Bobby, and with the rest of the little. . . But there we are.

The first slap hits Master Bobby high up, just above the right ear, and sends his chewing-gum splattering across the room. Number two comes back the other way – open-handed of course; I'm noted for my open-handed generosity – and Bobby gulps like the world has crumbled in his hands.

'Right,' I say. 'That's so that you understand that things are going to be a little different round here. Your mother has gone to the West Indies for a sudden six week holiday and I am looking after the house and everything in it. As long as that includes you, then you will not behave and talk like a Victorian navvy. I shall also talk to Faith and Charity later. Any questions?'

Although his face is still set in lines of accustomed misery and ill-temper, at least he talks less rudely. 'Yeah. Where's me chewing-gum gone?'

While he goes up to his bedroom to change out of his school-uniform into his jeans, I congratulate myself on my success so far. Much as I hate violence, there are times, and I reckon that was one of them.

With all the charm of a hacksaw blade running down glass, I hear a piercing whine from the hall. 'Mom! What's for me tea?'

It is Faith.

I call her in the living-room, and I spend nearly half an hour explaining to her exactly where Lobelia has gone, and when she'll be back, and how I'll be looking after them all for the next six weeks. I do it gently, because little Faith is somewhat less repulsive than her twin brother, and is regarded by her mother as very sensitive and delicate. I have my hankie ready for when she bursts into floods of tears, but she controls herself remarkably well.

'Is that it?' she asks when I reach the end of my little narration.

'Yes.'

'Right. What's for tea?'

I have not yet had time to go through the kitchen, but I spent long enough surviving my mum's cooking to have a rough idea of what not to do. Not that she was *that* bad. She once sees a travel film about San Francisco – I'm sure it was there because everyone was going around with flour in their hair – and it says about how fried ice-cream is a famous delicacy. Now I don't know much about cooking, but I do know it's not a good idea to drop a family block of Loganberry Ripple Cornish into a pan of boiling fat.

Still, as my old man said when we got rid of the fire brigade, we'd meant to have the kitchen decorated any way.

I can't wait to get in this kitchen, whipping up superb creations for the kids and for me. Maybe even a dinner party with canapés. Pronounced 'canapés'. Not can o'peas!

But just for tonight, as time has run out faster than a congregation of Scotsmen when the collection comes round, it will have to be something simple. Maybe even fish fingers. But just wait until I get organised.

I wonder whether to offer them that famous dish that I mention in one of my earlier epics. Oeufs aux tomates a Jonathan May. Eggs with tomato soup. I've come up with a variation on that for those food buffs among you. Instead of simply boiling the eggs and mixing them in, you can poach them in the Heinz's best tomato soup. I promise you there will be a most amazing effect.

I can't think of any way of mixing fish fingers and tomato soup, so I'll just fry them up with some bread and a tin of baked beans. Open a tin of sliced cling peaches and a tin of evap and we're away. Incidentally, I reckon they're called 'cling' peaches because one slice always clings to the side of the tin and you can't get it out. And it's dreadful when you can't get it out. Isn't it, missus?

I reckon that my explosion has cleared the air. Sort of new clear explosion. Bobby and Faith come down and eat their suppers with only the passing comment that they didn't know I was religious. I ask them why, and they say because I've served them a burned offering.

I hate bright kids.

Actually, I don't quite know how it happened, but the food is just a teeny bit scorched round the edges. While I am buttering the bread the fish-fingers singe slightly, and while I am scraping them the beans all get charred. While I am sorting them out of the saucepan, which reminds me I'd better buy another saucepan tomorrow, I catch the bread and butter with my elbow and it all falls on the floor. Butter side down.

While I'm picking that up, the fish fingers, that I've put back on to heat up start smoking like a chimney on fire.

Which reminds me of the time that Morrie is asked by a doctor whether he smokes in bed. 'Only if I forget the vaseline,' quips my merry brother.

Then the second tin of beans falls out of the automatic opener, landing all over the bread and butter that I've just scraped clean. I have to throw a wet cloth over the burning grill-pan. Wish I had my Uncle Nick, as he's a real wet blanket. I decide to throw away the bread and beans and butter and start again. Sadly, I forget that I've left the gas on under the grill and the wet cloth dries out and bursts into flames. I must remember to buy a new dish-cloth.

I beat this out with the floor-cloth, which also chars on the fringes. As do my fingers. Not to mention the fish's fingers that are blacker than my old man's collar.

The waste bin receives the whole thing.

I add floor-cloth to my list.

And a waste-bucket.

After that I . . . what? The waste-bucket? Well, the cloth wasn't quite extinguished and it set fire to the paper liner in the bucket.

The third tin of beans makes it safely as does the second lot of bread and butter. Apart from spilling some sugar on it, while brewing up the tea. But it takes me only a couple of minutes to scrape most of it off.

And a new kettle.

Don't they boil dry quickly! I hardly even turn my back on it before there is a dreadful smell of burning. I manage to get it out in the back garden alongside the waste-bucket and the grill-pan.

There is so much scorched metal and plastic out there it looks like the desert after the Seven Days War. Scorched earth isn't in it. There's also scorched crysanthenums and scorched dalia . . . chrismanthemumums . . . daylie . . . krismanthetetumumetums . . . flowers.

The third packet of fish fingers is the best. The second one? That went while I was removing the kettle.

Two new saucepans.

By Fanny and Delia! This cookery game isn't quite as simple as I thought. Or – dreadful thought – I have somehow inherited my old mum's unique way with food.

I'm not trying to keep giving you the idea of what a rotten cook my old mum is. But I remember that even she admitted that her malt bread wasn't quite what it should be. My old man fed some to his favourite pigeon, and took it up on the roof to launch it.

Dropped like a stone.

My old man went spare. Started to shout and hector. Our place got known as Hector's House.

But the kids eat what I finally serve up, and I pack them off up the stairs to get on with their homework. Two bedroom doors shut, and two trannies are switched on, and my ears are assailed by two loud versions of 'Love Your Baby, Kill Your Baby' by Mealy Plum, who are five spotty louts with a total age of thirty-seven, dressed in green velvet.

I have a few moments to relax after the labour of that meal. I think that I'll just close my eyes so that I can think more clearly about planning my household campaign.

Just close my eyes and think.

Just close my eyes and. . .

Just close my eyes. . .

Just close my. . .

Just close. . .

Just. . .

Zzzzzzzz!

That indicates the noise I make when thinking with my eyes shut.

I'm not asleep. Honest, I'm not. I need a comfortable bed to drop off properly. Did I ever tell you about the time that I tried to sleep in a water-bed? I didn't fancy it. All I got were wet dreams.

I dream that I can feel light hands caressing my body. Touching me on the knee. Rubbing softly up the outside of my thighs. Moving to the inside of my thighs. Fingers stroking me on my forehead. Cool, langorous. The hand on my thigh reaching closer. Edgar waking up to what's happening, and beginning to raise a smile.

This thinking with your eyes shut isn't bad. I'm certain that I'm awake, but I won't open my eyes and spoil this delicious illusion. The fingers are now at the top of my thigh. Stroking even higher. Shaking hands with Edgar, who is very pleased to meet them.

By George, G. and Gilman! Those dream fingers are tugging at the top of my flies, ready to pull it down and reach inside and hold...

'Leave him alone, you sneaky cow!!'

The voice is Faith.

The fingers are Charity's.

The embarrassment is mine, all mine.

'Go on, Carrie. Leave him alone.'

I should mention that Carrie is sometimes used in the Dugfondle household as a pet name for Charity. Not that she needs a pet name any more than a Black Widow spider does.

I am red of face, and swollen of Edgar. I don't know whether I am glad about Faith's interruption or not. If she hadn't come in when she did, then I might have done that which I would have enjoyed . . . I mean, regretted, for ever. But there is a song by the marvellous Doctor Hook about: 'Come on Carrie, carry me a little further.'

Charity can carry me as far as she likes any day.

If it wasn't for her mother.

Lobelia makes it very clear on my first day at number eighty-four, Copper Bottom, Withering Bumple, that her eldest daughter is strictly off-limits. And she gives me a graphic description of what will happen to me, and more specifically to Edgar, if I ever forget it.

There was something about branding-irons and blunt scissors!

So I move away from Charity's little hands, nearly knocking over the sofa in my hurry to get out of range. Faith stands in the doorway, her eyes registering every detail, like a supermarket detective. And with about as much sense of humour.

'Why don't you carry on upstairs, there's a good little girl, Faith,' I say, realising that my voice makes it sound as though I came last in a high-hurdles barbed-wire race.

'And let you carry on with Carrie downstairs! Not a chance, Jonny. I suppose it's all right if I call you Jonny, isn't it? Only some of Mummy's boy-friends like us to call them Uncle.'

'No. Jonny is just fine by me.' I shall find out more about these other boyfriends later. 'Now go on and get on with your homework. What is it?'

'The human genitals,' says the angelic child, not turning a blonde hair.

Such language! In my day, it was all birds and bees. The closest we ever got to sex was a picture of a rabbit's rumpoe and peering at a worm's willy through a microscope. The idea of actually talking about. . . Ugh! Men and women!! would have made old Miss Fanshawe (pronounced Featherstonehaugh) wet her navy blue bloomers.

I remember that Morrie once buys himself a pair of matched speakers and tells dad what good reproduction he's got. Dad makes him go upstairs and wash his mouth out with carbolic soap.

Finally, the two youngest are again busy growing deaf, and Charity and I are left together. As I did with Faith and Robert, I fill her in . . . sorry . . . tell her what's going on, and say that she'll be all right in my hands.

'I'm sure of that, Jonny. Did you like being in my hands then?'

Once again my face gives its famous impression of a cherry blancmange. 'Yes. No. I mean, possibly. But that's not the point.'

'I didn't miss the point then, did I Jonny? And look, there's the point coming up again.'

Damn Edgar! Letting me down like this. I must start wearing looser trousers.

'I bet Mum said that you had to make sure that I took my knickers off every night. Didn't she?'

The cherry blancmange merges into a pool of crimson lake. I manage a feeble grin and a nod of the head.

'Wouldn't you like to take them off, yourself, Jonny? Now?'

Of course not. The very idea.

No.

Charity sits down on the arm of the chair opposite, and deliberately lifts her skirt up. So that I can see the tops of her knees. She is wearing tights, I see with great relief. But they are those naughty tights that are designed to look like someone wearing stockings and suspenders.

Very slowly, like a pair of lock gates, she starts to open her legs, so that I can see higher and higher. I begin to feel a touch of vertigo.

Not a nasty skin ailment. That's impetigo. Vertigo. Means a fear of seeing ladies' knickers.

Well, it does to me.

'There you are, Jonny. Good job I put on one of my best pairs, isn't it?'

I feel as though someone has pushed a pair of garden shears down my throat and then opened them. I have lost my voice, and I don't know where to find it. I decide to leave it alone in the hope that it'll come home. But I worry about what it might have dragging behind it.

'You're not looking, Jonny. There. Can you see better now?'

I would have to be Lord Longford to avert my gaze at the vision. Charity leans further back and tugs her skirt up so high that I can see her eyebrows. She is one of the breed of young ladies who wear their pants outside their tights. I'm sure there's some interesting research to be done into why some wear them outside and some in. And I would love to volunteer for the job of chief researcher.

Charity's knickers are very small and very tight. In fact they would make a comfortable pair of trousers for a well-developed field-mouse. They are pale green in colour, and seem to be made of some sort of shiny material. Satin or silk.

She has a well-rounded figure does Charity, so I guess they are well sat-in.

'Do you like them, Jonny?'

I need inspiration. Unless the earth opens and swallows me up I have no way of knowing what might happen. I do, actually, but I dread those blunt scissors of Lobelia.

'Yes. They're quite...'

'Well, you know what Mummy said. You have to make sure that I take them off every night.'

The inspiration arrives. Lobelia has mentioned that Charity's fondest wish is to own a car of her own. Her eighteenth birthday is not far away.

'Your mother said that if you behaved properly for the whole six weeks, then she might buy you a car when she got back.'

The skirt drops faster than Crystal Palace. And I bid a fond farewell to those satin panties.

'She said she might?' There is a nasty stress on that word 'might'.

'No. Now you mention it, she actually said that she would. Definitely.'

Charity looks half disappointed that her fun has been spoilt and half pleased that her wish is going to come true at last. With a shrug of the shoulders she turns round and makes for the door.

'Jonny?'

'Yes?'

'Don't forget that I want some supper as well as the kids.'

Blast!

'And I'll try and be good. And I'll even remember to take off my knickers.'

'Good.'

'Just for you.'

Not so good.

But the evil moment has passed, and I am still safe from threats of retribution. Wearily, I go into the kitchen, which now resembles a soccer special train. I groan and reach for the fish fingers. There is a mirror by the cupboard, and I catch a glimpse of myself looking like death warmed up. I try a winsome smile.

And fail.

Oh well! Win some. Lose some.

Tomorrow's the first day of the rest of my life.

CHAPTER FIVE

Mrs. Vatman. Bright and early. The early worm that gets my goat.

'Managing all right?'

'Yes. Thank you, Mrs. Vatman.'

'Bet Lobelia took plenty of clothes with her on her holiday.'

'Yes. She did.'

Nosy git.

'Where did you say she'd gone?'

'West Indies.'

'Bahamas?'

'No. She doesn't wear them, but she's taken plenty of nightdresses.'

I can't say that I sleep all that well during my first night at eighty-four, Copper Bottom, Withering Bumple, without Lobelia. I imagine her sunning herself on a golden beach, and all I can do is toss and turn.

You have to turn afterwards, otherwise you roll in the sticky bit.

I finally lurch out of an uneasy sleep as the alarm clock shatters the morning. It was after midnight before I get to bed on that first night. There was the washing-up to get done. I reckon that a sand-blaster would have been of more use than super-incredibly-amazingly mild and gentle Puffo, the wonder washer. It may be gentle and kind to rubber gloves and all that, but it's damn-all use at washing up eight saucepans and four frying-pans.

Remind me to add them to my shopping list.

I stay up late to watch *Kojak*, which is my favourite programme after *Blue Peter* and *Magpie*, with the lovely Lesley and the lovely Jenny. I don't know what they're doing wasting such lovelies on teeny brats.

The bit in *Kojak* I manage to raise a weak smile at is where they're searching through New York phone books. One of them says: 'I'll take Manhattan,' and another one sings: 'The Bronx and Staten Island too.'

Ask your mum if you don't get it.

Trouble is with the Dugfondle television set; it's one of those little Japanese sets, and it is always on the blink. And I don't enjoy the *Grey and Grey Minstrel Show* at the best of times.

I have managed to send all three of the brood off to school and to work – Charity works in an accountant's office – with a square meal inside them. One round of toast each.

Mentioning accountants reminds me of the time that Aunty Rose worked for an accountant. This is before she meets Uncle Angus.

She goes in the office one day, with a bit of a swelling around the middle. Looks her boss straight in the eye, and says: 'Remember last year's squeeze?'

'Yes,' he says.

'Well,' says Rose, patting her stomach. 'I'm sorry to have to tell you that it's led to severe inflation.'

Actually, Adam was the very first accountant. He turned over a leaf and made an entry.

Lobelia said in her letter that she was sending me a longer letter describing the financial arrangements. Since my wallet is emptier than a salt-beef bar in Cairo, I can hardly wait.

There's all those saucepans. And more food. After last night and this morning, I have decided that I might have been a touch hasty in condemning some ladies' cooking. For a day or so I shall stick to the simple essentials. Like fish fingers and beans and frozen chips.

It is better to draw a long black veil over this morning's culinary disaster. The bacon vanished up its own smoky gammon. The fried eggs would make good blackboard rubbers. The tomatoes turned into a sort of thick red glue, which is fine if you want to stick some thick red bits of paper together but not much use otherwise.

The cereal is all right. Apart from the fact that I have used the milk to try and thin down the tomatoes, which results in a mixture so hideous that even I cannot face it.

(Publisher's Note: Hello. Remember me? I thought that it was such a long time since I'd cheered you up with my little appearances that I'd better just say a word here. I can tell you from personal experience that if Mister May couldn't face the food, then I swear that nobody could. One of the most painful experiences of my life was when I had to take Mister May to a good restaurant for a meal. I ordered coq au vin, and a nice Mouton Cadet with it. He ordered salmon with raspberry ice-cream and a coke and sherry!)

His memory is not quite right there. It was strawberry ice-cream. Thought it would stop him being such a food snob. He's the sort of bloke who'll send back the tablecloth if it isn't at the right temperature.

Bobby and Faith are a bit stroppy about this do-it-yourself instant nausea outfit that I serve up, but Charity has her double-barrelled sights set firmly on a new car, and quiets them down.

'I'm sure that Jonny is trying.'

'Very,' comments Bobby.

'Ha, Ha.' That's a hollow laugh from me. I mean to say, I haven't had any breakfast either.

But now it's eight forty-five, and there's time to sit down and relax.

Perhaps I could just sit down in this chair, and turn on some mindless drivel on the radio, and do a bit more of my closed-eye thinking.

I haven't got beyond the first Zzzz when there's a ring at the door. Knocking a cold cup of coffee all over my jeans, I make it to the front, and heave the door open.

'Morning Mrs Dugfondle. One pound fifteen. . . Blimey! You have changed.'

It took him long enough to look up, I think, wondering a little about what a high voice he's got. And I am not in the mood for funny-men.

'Yeah,' I snarl. 'I took a cheap-day return to Denmark and had an operation.'

There is a giggle. 'Sticks out a mile what a success it was.'

By Chilly and Winds! The old zipper has given up the ghost and there is Edgar scenting the morning air. And the milkman, as those of you who are still with me from the start will know, is no man.

At last our eyes meet, after I've tucked Edgar back into my purple male-huggers. And I am surprised. I recall that we had a lady milkman – a milklady – a female milk-person – when I lived in Great Barr, but she was nearly seventy, with the build of an all-in wrestler.

This lady is very different.

I've already given you a run-down on the way our relationship develops at the beginning of the book, so I won't go into a lot more detail now. Suffice it to say (I read that in a book writ by a proper writer of writ writings) that she – her name is Dolly – is a bit over five feet six tall, with a figure that even a serge uniform can't ruin. Is that pronounced 'surge' or 'sarge'? I'm never sure.

Anyway this Dolly, who is a mixture of good things, has the largest size in blouses and still has to keep the top three buttons undone. As she bends down to deposit the gold-tops on the step, I reel back from a view like gazing down the Grand Canyon. The view is heightened and the similarity too, by the fact that she doesn't wear a bra. And neither does the Grand Canyon.

I tell her about Lobelia, and she nods her head sympathetically. Which sets her Canyon into motion, revealing a couple of cherries bobbing about like coracles in a whirlpool. And that is something the Grand Canyon doesn't have.

'Poor old you. I suppose that means you'll be here all on your own, like?'

Am I imagining it, or is there a gleam of interest in those cornflower-blue eyes? She glances quickly up and down the street, but it is full early, and there's nothing stirring. Not even Mrs. Vatman's curtains.

'The fellow who had this round before me, reckoned that Mrs. Dugfondle was a bit of a . . . you know, goer. He said that she used to brighten up his morning round with a cup of tea and a bit of a nibble. Know what I mean?'

I do know what she means. Handy though it is to have somewhere to doss for a few weeks, even at the price of looking after the terrible trio, I am already getting the drift that Mrs. Dugfondle is a very merry widow indeed.

The milklady seems to be waiting for me to say something.

'Do I owe you something?' I ask, wondering if there is a bill to be paid.

'Well. I was just wondering if you were Mrs. D's fancy boy, or if the merchandise was available for anyone.'

'Merchandise! !' By the Lib and Fem! This is becoming too much. They'll be whistling at men in the street and pinching boy's bums in Tubes next.

I hope.

'Well. I don't know. What will the neighbours think if you suddenly start popping in for a quickie?'

'Your stock'll rise several points. And I hope that's not going to be all that rises.'

She has a ribald laugh. Unhealthy. Not to be confused with a ryvita laugh, which is healthy. And she digs me familiarly in the goolies with the blunt end of her felt-tip pen. And I felt the tip. Or my tip felt the felt-tip's tip.

So begins a relationship that continues on and off for the first part of my stay at eighty-four. Dolly is a good active start to the day, and helps me get out of bed faster than the best alarm clock.

Because it must be admitted that Jonny is not the best riser in the land. I reckon that God made the evenings, but the other bloke made mornings. If there is one thing that I hate more than most it's the early to rise and early to bed merchant. In my book – and this *is* my book – that usually makes a man healthy, wealthy and dead.

I rise most mornings feeling as though I've passed the night with my head buried in a grizzly's grotto. When the local paper arrives, the first thing I do is turn slowly to the obituary column to see if my name's in it.

Once I know it's not, I can get down to the business of surviving the day with better spirits.

And Dolly helps out a lot. She is warm-hearted. And warm-handed, which is surprising considering the freezing job she has to do, manipulating several hundred gallons of cows' left-overs. And she has a warm sense of humour.

And a warm . . . pretty well everything.

Dolly is a real gold-top bird, in every way.

One of the things I like best about her is the way she licks her lips afterwards. Like a big pussy that's just had the cream.

You know; I honestly never thought about it like that before.

The postman brings the awaited letter from the sun-bathing Lobelia, which reassures me of her love, and mentions again Charity and her damned knickers. There are the usual homely and affectionate details, like making sure I leave the garbage bin by the back gate on Mondays.

She has made arrangements with the local bank to send me thirty pounds, cash, each Monday to tide me over. As long as the tide doesn't turn I shall be all right. But I don't fancy keeping creditors at bay like King Canute. Who was, incidentally, a heavy drinker and gave birth to the expression about being as peed as Canute.

I sit for some time wondering what I'll have for my lunch. I wonder.

Zzzzzzzz.

I wonder what I'll have for tea.

Zzzzzzzz.

Supper.

By Mag and Pie! It's time to get the kids' tea, and I haven't been down the shops to get the new saucepans and food. I shall raid the cupboard and find some amazing selection of unthought-of delicacies for the little dear ones.

'Jonny?'

'What is it Robert?'

'This supper?'

'Yes?'

'Well. I was just wondering, if you don't mind; just wondering, what it actually was.'

'Why? Tastes all right, doesn't it?'

'No.'

That was Faith.

'Oh.'

That is me.

Actually, I have to own up and admit that I'm not all that amazed that it doesn't taste all that great.

Unusual? Yes.

Great? No.

But it is a measure of how successful a quick bunch of the fives round the ears can be with a child like Robert, who has been given his head for too long. And look what happens to people who get given their head. Like Charles Second. Or Salome First. After veil seven, that was.

The last thing that poor old John the Baptist saw before he got the chop was a veiled glance.

Returning to the children. The twins have clearly exchanged views and are going to be better behaved while I'm around. They aren't such bad kids, really. Not thought of a nasty revenge, or anything.

But the supper. It's a sort of stew. All I have left without a big hole in its bottom is one casserole and the budgerigar. So it has to be something like a stew.

(Publisher's Note: Normally I put in my witty comments and thoughts after Mister May has been allowed to have his say. But in this case I feel that I have a moral responsibility to you, the readers, to warn you that what is about to follow is unsuitable for children, or those of an unduly nervous disposition. I suggest that if you must read on, that you provide yourvelves with a large brown paper bag.)

Nit!

Although the paper bag reminds me of a trick I read about somewhere. Get on a plane, and carry with you a plastic bag filled with Russian salad. That gooey stuff with bits of chopped up egg and vegetables all mangled around in mayonnaise. Sit next to the most nervous person you can find. Wait until you're in the air, and pretend you're sick, and grab for the brown paper bag behind each seat. Make sick noises into it, and your neighbour will avert his gaze. Look the other way. Wait a few minutes, then put the bag, into which you have secretly transferred the Russian salad, on the floor.

Wait a few more minutes.

By now your neighbour will probably be feeling a little less than well. Comment you're feeling better, and pull out a spoon you have also put in your pocket before beginning the flight. Pick up the brown paper bag.

(Publisher's Note: Oh No! This isn't even the bit I was warning you about.)

Oh Yes!

Take the spoon and eat the Russian salad out of the brown

paper bag. I guarantee you will have an empty seat next to you for the whole journey.

Actually, I shouldn't make jokes about being travel sick. As you know, I am about the world's worst traveller. I'm the only person in the history of British Airways to be treated for air sickness while still on the bus driving to the plane.

This stew.

Lobelia hadn't exactly left her cupboard bare, but then again it wasn't overflowing with plenty like Margaret Thatcher's larder. She has a very conservative selection, does Mrs. Thatcher.

The Dugfondle supply centre contains three tins of celery. One tin of cream of scampi soup. Six packets of lentils. Half a pound of self-raising flour. That's jammed at the back of the cupboard, but I use a bit of shelf-raising power and get it out.

Three shabby sticks of rhubarb that look as though they've been there for some months. I chuck them in, leaves and all. A tomato that has a few odd white spots. Not unlike South Africa. But these are furry. A jar of mixed herbs. A half-empty tin of evaporated milk. A full tin of custard powder. Powder to the people, Oh yeah.

Eight different bottles of sauce, none of them with more than a crusty half-inch in them. But I wash them all out with some Australian sherry I find in the cupboard under the stairs and empty the lot in.

The kitchen is smelling like Uncle Angus when he got a job working down the sewers, clearing out the blockages. He does quite well at it, and after two years they give him a broom and shovel.

What it needs is something to give it a bit more body, so I swill out seven old jam-jars with the dregs of some vinegar and heave that in, stirring well, clothes-peg jammed over my hooter. A sliced loaf is in the bread-bin, but it does not appear to be quite new. As I throw in the grey slices, I notice that one or two of them have a light blue, feathery sort of growth attached to them. Penicillin is good for you so that can't be going to do any harm.

It's not a proper stew without meat, and fortunately Mrs. Vatman feeds her Alsatian close to the hole in the fence, so a tin and half of Cheerychum goes bubbling in the mixture.

Five Chocoroonies, four Weetitums, three Sunnycorns, two Countrymix and a partridge in a pear tree top things off well.

I don't know what it does to the kids, but by the gods it terrifies me.

A day that begins amazingly well with the radiant Dolly, ends less well when Charity comes in during supper and turns green at the sight of the gunk the twins are shovelling down and flees to her room, hand clasped over her mouth.

Well, tomorrow is another day, and I shall *really* begin to get this housework and shopping bit tied up.

It would help if I could sleep well. But the bed is a vast queen-sized one, and I can still detect the feminine odours of Lobelia. Odour, what can the matter be?

I have a very odd dream. No, not that kind of odd, dear. Funny peculiar.

I dream that I am a cowboy, and I have just ridden into a frontier town. The sheriff there, who bears an uncanny resemblance to my Uncle Angus, greets me and invites me into the saloon. Which is called the 'Cheat and Ham'. What a very strange name for a saloon!

'Where's the action round here, sheriff?' I ask. 'I been three months on the range with only sheep to look at and I aim to get me a woman.'

'Sorry, sonny,' says the bewhiskered old fool of a sheriff. 'All we've got is Ed the barman.'

'I ain't like that,' I protest, ordering myself another snort of Doctor Pepper.

'Sorry, about that.'

'Come on now. There just must be some sort of naughty

action around this here one-horse town. Dang my britches if there mustn't.' In my dreams I fear that I am remembering too many Hopalong Cassidy movies.

'Nope,' spits the sheriff. 'Just old Ed the barman. That's all.'

'I keep telling you, I ain't like that at all.'

I down another slug of red-eye, whatever that is. Sounds like the sort of drink that gives you conjunctivitis.

'I'll be hornswoggled if I ain't a burstin' for some female company.' The Gabby Hayes look is in this year.

The sheriff looks at me out of eyes that have seen too many Tequila sunrises and too many long hours in the dusty corridors of Central Casting.

'I keep tellin' you, you young whippersnapper. There ain't a single female in this here town. The best we can offer you is Ed the barman.'

Finally, and do remember this is in my dream, I go back to the marshal and thump him in the back disturbing the red dirt of a thousand Mohave mornings and several hundred hours of the wardrobe department. 'All right then, sheriff. Seeing as how I'm plumb desperate, I'll go along with you. But just how many folks will know about it?'

'Seven.'

'Seven!'

'Seven.'

'Why seven? I keep telling you, sheriff, that I really ain't like that, anyway. I don't want folks getting the wrong idea.'

'There has to be seven, son.'

'Why?'

'You and me.'

'That's two.'

'Ed himself.'

'That's three.'

'And the four guys we need to hold Ed down, 'cos he ain't like that either.'

CHAPTER SIX

I wake up soaking wet with sweat, after one of the worst nights I can remember.

And being dripping like that reminds me of the time that my Uncle Nick decides to take up tap-dancing.

He falls in the sink.

I bet that lots of you reckon that this book is going to turn into a chapter of dreadful culinary accidents, interspersed with moments of pure naughtiness.

Close.

As far as this particular chapter is concerned, it is not an unfair comment.

To begin at the beginning. After a night that leaves my eyes feeling like hot humbugs, I decide that an early breakfast is what everyone needs. Go to the kitchen, and find that there is a ridiculous shortage of saucepans and things. How can Lobelia have managed with such sparse equipment? Actually, some of her equipment is very un-sparse.

I conveniently forget the mound of festering scrap metal in the back garden, looking like the leftovers from Lord Beaverbrook's wartime appeal for old pots and pans to make into Spitfires.

It is not an easy breakfast. Have you ever tried to cook porridge in a frying-pan?

I must buy another frying-pan. They don't make them very strong, do they? Turn your back for a minute and there's a mess of porridge gradually turning into tar.

Both Faith and Bobby turn up their noses at it, and I have to admit that I don't altogether blame them for that. But they can both do with losing a little weight. Ready for the epicurean (look it up. I did) feast that I shall commence on as soon as I get things together.

Both of them trundle off to school with faces longer than a wet week in West Bromwich. Which, incidentally, is where I was born. Which brings me to the matter of the birthday card that I received this year. I used to give you an odd mention of famous birthdays, and told you that mine is the same day as Horace Walpole. And two fine lads actually looked it up and I get a card from Duke and Blue. Thanks a lot lads. For those of you who can't be bothered to look it up, it's the twenty-fourth of September. So don't miss it again.

Charity also appears for breakfast, having done even worse than the unheavenly twins last night. But it doesn't seem to have done them any harm. I leave the pot containing the rest of the stew out in the garden and this morning there are five dead sparrows, a blackbird, three mice, a rat and a large ferret, all stiff and cold round the stiff, cold mixture.

'There must be something to eat,' moans the beautiful young girl. I could do with more of the beauty and less of the moans. Perhaps I should nickname her Moana Lessa.

'I can't see anything around here that I'd like to eat,' inadvertently laying myself open for the sucker punch.

'How about me, Jonny?' asks Withering Bumple's answer to Lolita, placing one bare foot on the kitchen table, and hitching up her skirt to reveal another pair of those thin, scanty, tight, silken, panties.

If you'll pardon the expression, Charity is offering it to me on a plate. But those blunt scissors loom large again, and I shake my head and try to think of algebra and other boring subjects. Anything to keep Edgar's mind off those panties, and that tantalising tendril of curlylocks that peep out the side.

I am beginning to realise how hard Edgar is going to find the next few weeks. Or should that be how hard I am going to find Edgar for the next few weeks?

'Listen, Charity.'

She cocks her head on one side and assumes an exaggerated listening position. 'Can't hear a thing, Jonny, darling.'

'I mean listen to me. Listen. Listen. Listen to me.'

I should note that that last bit is for the benefit of the Buddy Holly fans, as it's a line from one of his songs.

'I'm listening.'

She has a habit, as do many monks. No, she has this habit of poking her tongue out at the corner of her mouth, and then running it slowly over her full, ripe . . . lips, and grinning at the same time. I find it rather off-putting. Not to mention a bit on-turning.

'Well. I'm going to go shopping this morning, and then things will get better.'

'Forgive me for saying it, Jonny, but they couldn't get much worse. I haven't seen so much burned food since the fire at the Chinese Takee-Outee.'

'Fair comment. I'm nothing but fair, Charity, and that is a fair comment.'

Thinks: 'Wonder how she'd like a mouthful of knuckle.'

'If there's nothing to nosh, then I might as well push off to the station.' Only she doesn't actually say 'push off'. 'I'll get a sandwich at Liverpool Street station.'

That is something that I would not wish on my worst enemy. A British Rail sandwich. Two slices of old, dry bread, being forcibly held apart by a slice of old dry cheese, served with that cheerful indifference that typifies the great days of the Spanish Inquisition.

I have just thought of a worst enemy that maybe I would wish that on. And I am not thinking of my brother, Morrie. There is one other, whose name I cannot remember. Perhaps it will come back to me while Charity takes her trip to London down the Lea Valley.

I have to make two journeys to the shops. The first is to buy an array (an array's a laugh) of pots and pans and a washing-upper-doer thing, with some rubber gloves to save my lily-whites from getting frayed at the edges with all this toiling away over a hot sink.

I shall never forget hearing my old man talking to some of his mates about housework. 'No trouble in my place,' he boasts through his National Health dentures. 'I've got a marvellous gadget. I screw it on the bed and it does all of the work.'

'What's it called?' asks one of his mates.

'The old woman,' he replies.

I must say that I'm not all that impressed with this non-stick linings business in pans. As I'm also feeling a touch on the peckish side myself, I force down a couple of salad rolls from the Millpond Cafe on the corner of Copper Bottom. And the newsagent has just one half pound box of Black Magic left, and it looks lonely on the shelf by itself, so I put it out of its misery.

Then back home to try out one of the new saucepans. There is still some custard left in the cupboard after my stew, so I decide that my first experiment will be a simple one. I follow the instructions very carefully, though I fear that I have confused a teaspoon and a tablespoon. We don't have all these sophistications at home in Great Barr. There are three kinds of spoons. Big, small and the green one that is used for Gran's medicine. It was silver until Gran started using it to take her medicine.

I turn the custard around with a wooden spoon like it says on the tin, but it remains obstinately thin and milky. I like my custard rich and thick. Like my marmalade. I once go out with this girl who's into psychology and all that. I tell her about my food tastes, and she says it's all part of my gizmo. Or something that sounds like that. (Could she have meant machismo?)

While I watch this turgid mixture still refusing to get all nice and creamy, there is a ring at the door. I go and answer it, and it is the postman with the usual selection of merry bills.

I think I must enter a time warp (warpsadaisy) because I can only be talking to him for a couple of minutes at the outside. Well, I'm not going to invite the postman for a couple of minutes chat on the inside, am I?

'Got something cooking, have you?' he asks with that nasty grin that people use when they know there's something going wrong. I used to see it on Morrie's face when he hears a great crash from the kitchen, and goes in to ask mum if anything's broken. He *knows* something's broken, and he just sort of pretends to be concerned.

Postman doesn't mean that he thinks there's something cooking. He means that he knows there's something burning. I hope the Alsatian across the road at 'Mon Repos' gets him.

The custard has thickened all right.

Shame there's no market for smoky yellow round bricks these days.

Still, I must learn to look more on the bright side. I shall use this as a fine chance to test the non-stickery part of the saucepan. The amber ashes in the slightly melted oval saucepan will be perfect.

Welcome to the ashes test at the oval.

It doesn't come off all that easily, but I find a sheet of sandpaper under the sink, and I use that to clear it. After a lot of hard scraping, the custard is all gone. And I guess it won't hurt the nonstickiness of the pan.

The postman goes past on his old bike with a cheery wave of the hand. He is an amazing-looking man. Copper-coloured hair, steel-blue eyes, bronze skin and a silver moustache. A man of mettle!

Shopping.

Which reminds me of a small jest about two old maids who go shopping together. Down to the local green-grocer for their fruit and vegetables.

On the counter is this pile of enormously long and fat cucumbers.

Wait for it, you dirty-minded crew!

One old maid looks at the other old maid, and points at the cucumber and winks. Second old maid winks back.

'How much is a cucumber?' asks the first old maid.

'They're fifteen pence each, dear, or three for thirty pence.'

Old maids look at each other. First old maid turns back to greengrocer. 'Very well. We'll take the three for thirty pence.'

Second o.m. nudges her. 'I suppose we can always eat the other one.'

I can see that without Lobelia here, life will still not be a monastic round. There's Dolly the milk, and I reckon that at least half the ladies of Withering Bumple would do a turn if pressed. And I wouldn't mind pressing some of them!

Thinking of the monastic life reminds me of the time that Uncle Angus has had enough of Aunt Rose, and decides that he's going to be a monk. Reads books about it. Then decides not to do it. Uncle A. is not overly fond of washing, and he reads all about the ablutions of the monasteries and reckons they aren't for him.

I was going to tell you about going shopping.

I am still going to tell you about going shopping, so stop trying to sneak a few pages further on, looking for the dirty bits.

There is a reasonable choice of shops in the village. Several small grocers. And one very tall one.

There is also a supermarket. Well, actually, it is not all that super. Clark Kent wouldn't be seen dead in it. Not that Clark Kent (being Superman for those four people in the world who don't know) could be seen dead anywhere. And that's a kryptonic remark.

The money from the bank has arrived and I fold the six crisp fivers in my hand, and set off. I have been pouring over my Daily Mirror – it soaks it up better than anything else – and am all genned up on what to buy and what not to buy. I shall avoid all those silly special offers that tempt housewives to waste their precious money on things that they don't either want or need.

Nobody makes a fool of Jonny May, folks.

Listen.

Please.

Stop giggling, and listen.

All I want to know is does anyone want to buy off me sixteen bottles of malt vinegar, and forty-six light bulbs?

Well, they were so cheap!!!!!!!

I walk in and my ears are bombarded with the boring strains of canned music. Played by Alberto Piranha and his Sparkhill Senores. The shop is brightly-lit, with an array of signs like Spaghetti Junction. What I don't understand, and I'm not trying to make excuses for the vinegar and bulbs, is why nothing is ever the right price.

Either it's 'Special Offer – five pence off' or it's 'Two pence off recommended price'. How on earth do I know what the recommended price is? Might be a hundred pounds. Might be ten pence.

And the advertising. 'Cleans better'. Better than what? Blancmange?

I do some shopping, apart from the vinegar and the lights. Well, I keep telling you; they were a special offer, and it seemed an offer I couldn't refuse.

The first counter is manned by a pimply youth. When I cough to attract his attention his eyes light up like dead cod, and he becomes enthused with supreme indifference.

'Yeah?'

'I want some soap powder.'

'Why?'

I do not think this is any of his business, so I try a bit of banter. Better banter than batter.

'Wash my smalls with.'

'Poof.'

'What?'

'Nothin'.'

'Well?'

'What?'

Those of you who have stuck with me through other adventures, both of you, will know that I am not a great hero. He who doesn't fight but runs away, lives to run away another day, like my old man used to say.

But there are times when the fighting blood of the Mays is roused. Remember that I am one of the Great Barr Mays. Not one of the Hampton Court Mays!

I lean across the glass top, suspended over row upon row of pale pink sausages. The youth is wary, but is reassured by my smile. I beckon him with my finger. He leans forward, his face looking like a map of the moon in close-up.

'Wadjerwant?'

'See these sausages?' I ask, my smile becoming even broader, like an army recruiting sergeant explaining that square-bashing doesn't go on any longer.

'Yeah.'

'Try that act on with me again, smiley, and I shall take them all, and I mean *all*, and ram them right up your repulsive jacksie. Get the message?'

While telling him this I maintain my smile, and grab him by the collar, twisting it hard, so that his face resembles a swollen grape. Only when his tongue hangs out do I let go, and gently brush him down.

'Right?'

'Croak, croak.'

'What?'

'Cough, choke.'

'It's no choking matter, smiley. Now just tell me where the soap powder is.'

'Behind potted meats and before salad cream,' he gasps, looking at me with a mixture of fear and hatred. As long as the first outweighs the second, I couldn't give a flying monkey's about it.

There is rather a sweet little girl wandering round, seemingly in charge of that area, and I walk up to her. Before I open my mouth, she opens hers, and points at me, somewhere in the region of Edgar, her face a mask of horror.

Before she speaks, my fingers fly to make sure that my million hasn't gone zip, but all is snug. What can be wrong? She looks like I'm a nettle in a nudist colony.

'Little basket!' she cries.

'I know, but I'm rather lovable when you really get to understand me,' I reply, quicker than you-know-who doing a dive in the penalty area.

'No. Little basket,' she repeats.

All these repeats. Worse than I.T.V. summer schedules. Or the Beeb's if you want fairness.

'You ain't got a little basket!' she bellows, like my Aunt Holly when at the zoo and an elephant steps on her toe. It was in the path. The toe-path. The beast also plopped on her parasol which added a lot of insult to a fair amount of injury.

'No, I haven't. I am always very careful about things like that,' I reply.

'Iris means you have neglected to collect a trolley to transport your wares,' interrupts a gloomy man in a long white smock, who I take to be the manager. He looks like a refugee from that T.V. series about a mortuary attendant. *Playing It Ghoul*. That one.

Of course! I have seen enough films of these places, and spotted the ladies bustling around like Niki Lauda cutting corners. I take one out and move back to Iris, who is busy on a major excavating job on her right nostril.

'Soap powder, please?' I ask.

She uses her left hand to point vaguely behind her. 'What size you want?'

'Ordinary,' I say.

You'd have thought that I'd asked for the lost treasure of the Incas. Her jaw drops with an audible click, and her right hand falls limply from her nose.

'We ain't got that size.'

'All right. What size have you got?'

'All right, Iris. I'll deal with this customer, thank you.'

Doctor Doom is back.

'I just want an ordinary size packet of soap powder,' I say feebly. I never reckoned it would be as difficult as this. Now I know why so many housewives go around with faces longer than a wet motorway.

'What brand?'

'Lazy Y. Flying Q. Double Diamond. Bar B.Q.,' I say, trying for a light tone.

And failing.

Had I gobbed on his shining tiles I would have got as warm a reception.

'What brand of powder?'

'What's the difference?'

For the first time, a faint smile ghosts across his mouth, with its head tucked under its arm. 'Between you and I, sir, there is neither a jot nor any tittle between them. Some do slightly better in certain areas of the wash than others, but they are all more or less the same.'

This is what I have long suspected, and it comes as no kind of surprise to me. Like I say, these housewives are so easy to con. Whoops! Forgot for a minute there about the vinegar and light bulbs.

'What size, sir?'

'Twelve inches,' I snap out, unthinkingly.

'I am not talking about your collar size, sir,' says the Master of Misery.

Nor am I.

Which reminds me of a risky risqué joke, but I will save it to the end of the chapter. Something to look forward to, like.

(Publisher's Note: Here I am. I shall check the joke out very carefully, so you can rest assured it will not be in the least distasteful.)

Don't worry, folks. Since he's fired that lovely leggy secretary with the snakeskin shoes, he's got nobody to explain the naughty bits to him.

'I don't mind. Just ordinary sort of size for a family wash.'

There is a gleam in his eyes, like Elizabeth Taylor's safe-deposit box. 'Family size. You want the family size.'

That makes it sound to me like big.

'That sounds to me like big.'

'No such size as big. We have Family. Jumbo. Super. Extra. Massive. And Large.'

'Oh.'

'Large is smaller than Massive, but bigger than Jumbo. Jumbo is much bigger than Family but slightly smaller than Extra. Super is the same as Jumbo, but it's in a long flat box instead of a short thick box.'

I feel my brain beginning to fray at the edges. At the corners of my ears, I recognise that Carlos Piranha is plucking out *The Bonny Banks of Loch Lomond*, as a samba.

He presses a duo-pack of Family size in my trolley, which means I spend an extra forty-five pence to save one half penny for the double purchase. I notice that it is also called the 'Euro-size Five-B'.

The rest of the shopping goes better, though I have the same sort of problem with eggs. I want small eggs, which I discover are called standard, while the middle-size eggs are called large, and there's no such thing as large eggs.

On the way I become hypnotised by all the blazing signs, and find myself trapped into this ludicrous situation where I fill my basket with vinegar and light bulbs.

I realise now why my mum used to paper the breakfast table with notes reminding her of things she needed to get at the shops. My mind goes blank at the row after row of goodies, and I can't remember what we need. Apart from the fact that it's more or less everything.

Obviously, being a sensible and highly-intelligent person, I only get the basic necessities that will see us through until my next visit to the shops the same time next week. That is one of the facts about housewives that I have never understood. Why they find it necessary to go to the shops more or less every day of the week. Lobelia has a freezer, and there is also a reasonable sized fridge.

I shall not have to go to the shops again until . . . tomorrow.

Damn it!

Seven tins of pineapple chunks. Four bottles of ketchup. I'll ketch up with them later. Nine jars of black olives. I hope Olive doesn't miss them. A loaf of bread. I used my loaf about that particular item. Various jams. I'm always getting into those. Bottle of orange squash. Eggs. Butter. One of each. Coffee. Chocolate.

I'll cut this boring list short.

No. Actually, that's the whole list, and I am aware thank you very much, that there are a few essentials missing from it. But there's always tomorrow.

Faith and Bobby are both out for their supper tonight, so I shall whip up a little something for myself. Charity is going to the flicks to see a film about a man-eating measle. Called *Sores.*

Perhaps a soufflé. Or perhaps a little pasta dish. The trouble with a pasta dish is that it has no futura.

On the other hand, maybe I'll open one of the cookbooks I have bought this afternoon. I like the look of this one. *Cooking for the Human Garbage-Disposal Unit* by someone called John B. Harvey. Obviously a pen-name. Real name's probably Johnny B. Goode.

There's a recipe in here that I like. It's called the Casserole au Porc. Which either means a pork casserole, or a casserole for pigs. It's difficult to guess which. As I have no pork, I shall have to substitute some eggs and bread. And as I lack the wherewithal (what a silly word that is. Where with all!) to make the sauce, I shall almost certainly use a tin of tomato soup that I find has somehow attached itself to my person.

Now. Let me see.

'Take the pork, and shred it into fine pieces, scattering them in the bottom of the casserole.'

Haven't got any meat, so the bread'll have to do.

I'll keep the eggs for a bit.

'Prepare the sauce with the basil, fennel, bechamel, cream, butter, garlic and other ingredients as shown as on page twenty-seven.'

This haute cuisine is dead easy. No trouble at all. As I don't have all that foreign muck, I shall take the trusty opener in the right hand, and the can of Heinz tomato soup in the left. Open it and pour into a saucepan.

'The mushrooms and petit pois should be simmering in the oven.'

Maybe they should, but they aren't. I wouldn't know a petit pois from any other kind of pois.

Looks like the eggs, so I pop them on and cook them for three minutes from the moment the water comes to the boil. Nice and soft with firm whites.

I don't have a casserole so the rest of the recipe is a bit pointless. Perhaps if I just pour the soup in over the bread and then place the eggs delicately on top of the whole and then stir into one sticky fershlugginer mess, it will be more or less what this Harvey bloke had in mind.

It's delicious.

Wonderful.

Lip-smacking good.

This cordon bleu is a doddle, I tell you. Like I say, the housewife's job is dead easy, when you use your loaf. And a few eggs and a tin of soup.

But I still wish that someone would take a few of these bottles of vinegar off my hands. Or some of the light bulbs. Please.

I haven't forgotten. A naughty joke connected with the length of my . . . neck measurement.

My sister Melanie, on whom many sons have set, once goes out with this rich nutter. Called the Honourable Ffreddie Ffortescue Ffitz-Nnolan.

Has everything, but he lusts after my sister. Not surprising. When she's all dolled up she looks like Twiggy, only much more so, if you know what I mean.

But Melanie doesn't fancy him. His armpits aren't his charmpits, or something. So she thinks up a way of putting him off, and stopping him pestering her to marry him.

'I'll marry you, Ffreddie,' she says, 'on two conditions. Right?'

'Wwhat aare tthey, oold tthing?' aasks Ffreddie.

'I promised my dying mum that I would only marry a man with a Lamborghini car.'

'Yes?'

Sorry. I mean: 'Yyes?'

'And a twenty-four inch spam ram.'

'Ttwenty-ffour iinch?'

'Right.'

Off goes Ffreddie, and Melanie reckons she's got rid of him for good. Week later there's a roaring noise outside our house and there's Ffreddie in a bright red Lamborghini. Leaps out and embraces Melanie.

'Tthere wwe aare. Nnow wwe ccan gget mmarried.'

'What about the twenty-four inch spam ram?' asks my sweet sister.

Ffreddie beams. 'Nno pproblem. Mmy ddoctor ssays hhe ccan ccut aan iinch ooff.'

I'm not trying to keep you reading, or anything like that, but the next chapter will have some very naughty confessions of a window-cleaner. Like nothing you've ever read anywhere else before.

Promise.

CHAPTER SEVEN

Don't think that my family are all a lot of layabouts and sex maniacs and crooks. Not all of them. For instance; my Uncle Nick has a wonderful war record.

It's Flanagan and Allen singing 'Run Rabbit Run'.

Two weeks have passed.

And, yes, things are getting better.

It's a rare day when I burn anything, and I'm actually venturing into the fields – taking care where I tread – of real cooking. Bobby and Faith are as good as I could expect, but living with them is still a bit like waiting for a bomb to explode. They still resent me being there and their dear Mummy not being there. But they have enough sense to know that none of us have a lot of choice.

But in four more weeks, Lobelia will be back.

I've had a card from her. Showing a beach of amazing whiteness. A sea of amazing blueness. And a sunset of amazing redness. The only thing that isn't amazing is grace. The grace of the overweight native dancer in the foreground. The message is short.

'Lots of ups and downs, but there are several lovely men showing me all the ins and outs. See you in a month. And make sure that Charity keeps taking her knickers off.'

She does.

Despite all my efforts to restrain her, Charity still flaunts her nearly naked body about the house. Particularly on the odd occasions that she and I are on our own in the place. So far I have been able to keep myself under control. But there are four more weeks.

And Dolly is also on holiday.

So where is Jonny going to go to have a nice time?

My ideas about the local housewives are not working out. I think that they all know each other so well, that none of them dares to make a move. Particularly the lady across the way, who divides her time between failing the driving test, and falling off the curtain rail and breaking her telescope.

And the work of running the house? I hear you ask. I am of a mind to tell you to mind your . . . but I agree that it may be a fair question. And I shall answer it.

Firstly, the shopping.

This is now going like a dream.

Well, a nightmare is a sort of dream, isn't it?

You don't happen to know anyone who wants to take one hundred and eight plastic tulips off my hands, do you?

Actually, it's not too bad. I now manage quite regularly to boil the breakfast eggs without burning the saucepan. And half a loaf is better than none anyway.

Nothing now gets too badly scorched, though at some breakfasts there are more cases of singe than at a Sikh party.

Like the lady who sat on the bacon slicer, I am finding I am getting behind with my orders.

Despite pressure from the children, I insist that they wash most of their own clothes and do the ironing, as this is something that I cannot possibly cope with. But there is a big pile of Lobelia's clothes, and a basket full of mine that really could do with washing. But I never seem to have the time to do them.

So, as soon as Charity has left for work, I shall do some shopping, and then pop off to the launderette round the corner. I have noticed that nobody ever goes in there until the afternoon on a Wednesday, as they are all going into the nearest town for the market.

By Butt and Tock!

'Go and get ready for work! You can't come rushing down the stairs like that with no clothes on at all.'

Charity is bare-naked. Bouncing, and I do mean bouncing, across the kitchen.

She comes over and stands pressed up against me, where I have backed into the corner by the fridge. Her twin-fronted chest is pressed so close to me that her knobs are creasing my Duane Eddy tee-shirt.

She runs her fingers down the picture of the boss guitar man, until she finds my navel under it, and begins to play her game on a lower level.

'Sorry, Jonny, darling. But I was in such a hurry this morning to get dressed that I quite forgot to put any clothes on.'

I get rid of her without too much risk from the blunt scissors, and smack her bottom, sending her giggling back to her room to slip into a supremely short skirt and blouse. I don't know how I shall hold out against her for the next four weeks.

After she's gone I feel the need for a cold shower, which does me a load of no good, but at least means I can walk down Withering Bumple High Street without too much embarrassment.

I wave my good mornings to the ladies down Copper Bottom. The shopping bag packed with Lobelia's and my clothes is damnably heavy. I buy my Mirror, which I think reflects events better than other papers, and stroll round to the launderette. To my disappointment, the lady who runs it, a jolly lady in her fifties – and I'm not talking about her age – is just shutting the front door.

'Are you closing up?' I ask.

'No dear. I always open up by putting a "Closed" sign on the front door.'

She is about as jolly as the Black Death.

'Oh. I've only got one wash to do, and I wondered if you. . .' I let the sentence dangle like a politician's promise.

'Well. . . If you promise to lock up again afterwards, then I suppose it won't matter, dear. I never get anyone in this time of day.'

And she pushes off. What a nice lady! you are thinking. To let Jonny in. She agreed so quickly.

She also tucks the pound note quickly away into her pocket.

But I am in, and that's the main thing.

I unpack the bag, grateful that there is nobody else there to see me. Lobelia seems to get all her undies through those small ads in the papers. 'Cleo – exotic half-cup bra with wet-look panties and sheer black stockings. To put life in the man in your life.'

You know the sort of thing I mean.

There is also a strange exotic nightdress that seems to be made out of three yards of feathers and four inches of black ribbon.

I bung them all in one of the machines, and pile my Y-Fronts and tee-shirts and jeans and socks into another. Shove in the powder and off we go. At this point I notice that this morning's breakfast has left its mark on me in more ways than one. The fried peanut butter sandwich burst in my hands and has left a nasty stain on my other pair of jeans. The ones I wear as opposed to the ones spinning round in the machine.

There is a dryer that works most efficiently, so I decide to take a chance. Lock the door, and strip right off and throw everything in a third machine. The dryer will make sure they are all nice to put back on and go home again.

So far so good. Out comes the flimsies and in the dryer. Whirl, zoom – sexier than colour telly – and click, out they come, ready to wear.

I have just pulled out all my clobber, soaking wet and bubbly – like an earwig in a glass of champagne – when the phone rings. Naked as a peeled tomato, I answer it, nearly slipping on the steamy floor. It is the lady who runs the joint.

She has news.

Not good news.

BAD NEWS!!!!!!!!

I feel a bit trembly, just thinking about it, so it's better if I give you the whole of the conversation. Just bare, I mean bear, in mind that I have no clothes on at all, and that there are a pile of dry frillies in the bag, and a mound of soaking clothes of mine just ready to go in the spin-dryer.

'The spin-dryer.'

'What about it?'

'Don't use it?'

'Why not? Anyway, I've already used it once.'

'Oh, that's fine then dear. But it only works once, then the belt-drive jams and it won't work again for about five hours when it cools down. There's a man coming this afternoon. That's why I was closing it down.'

'Aaaaaaaaaaaaarrrrrrrgggggghhhhhh!!! Why didn't you tell me before, you silly great...?'

'Forgot, dear. Anyway, you did want me to let you in, didn't you? Must go. The pips are coming. Byeeee.'

She gives me the pip.

What? What am? What am I? What am I to do?

It is still quiet outside, as I wipe off some of the steam from the window. Maybe I could gather the clothes round me and make a run for it. There's only about three hundred yards to the safety of eighty-four Copper Bottom.

I wonder about trying on the wet jeans, but they are turning colder and clammier than my mum's sponge cake. But there isn't any alternative.

Well...

That flimsy nightie is nice and dry and warm, and it will just about cover up my essentials in case I run into any ladies. I'm all in favour of decent exposure, but in the right place and at the right time.

I try it on, feeling one of the right berks. It covers up Edgar, but the thing is transparent, and the feathers are no protection. Still. It's better than nothing. I decide to make a run for it, with just Lobelia's frillies in the bag, and put on my oldest pair of jeans back at the house and return for the other clothes later. They'll slow down my dash too much. And I am well known as a dashing fellow.

There is a ribbon for a belt and I knot it around my muscular stomach. Hard and lean, that's me.

(Publisher's Note: Lard and mean, I'd say.)

Tee bleeding hee.

Slide the bolt on the door and bolt.

Nobody on the street. Off the shopping area, and up Copper Bottom. Still nobody. I hear a door open a few houses on the left, and then shut. My heart sinks lower than Linda Lovelace's tonsils, but it is only someone taking in the milk. Round the next corner, feeling chilly round the willy, and I shall be safely...

'Hello, hello, hello.'

I bet he says: 'What's all this then?'

'What's all this then?'

I win the bet, but lose the race.

'Come on sir. Or is it madam?'

There is one thing I like less than a miserable policeman and that is a happy policeman. This is the local copper who does actually live in Copper Bottom with his wife and three little ferrets. He drives a very chi-chi panda car.

'I can sexplain nothing, potifer,' I find myself saying. Those trusty friends who have stuck with me through thick and thin in other adventures will remember that my mind has this habit of slipping a few cogs when the chips are down and I am in the soup. My publisher tells me that is a mixed metaphor. I'm surprised as I never mix metaphors with pleasure.

'What?'

'Who heard. I mean I heard. Hard. I can tell you a lot about it.'

'Lot of lies, I expect.'

He has reached down and pulled out his thing . . . notebook, and is currently licking his other thing . . . pencil, to take down all of my particulars, which are unprotected.

'No. A pack of truth. It's like this coccifer. I mean, stunstable. I mean. . .'

I am saved from further trouble, by him waving a finger the size of a pork chop at me. Rather a pork chop than a karate chop.

'Be easier if you give me your name and address first, then we'll know who we're talking to.'

'I'm May.'

(Publisher's Note: There was a joke here, or what Mister May likes to think of as being a joke, and I have decided in my infinite wisdom that it will speed the narrative if I remove it. That's all; carry on.)

The only wisdom he's got is in a glass by his washbasin.

Anyway, we'll carry on like he says.

'No officer. Jonathan May.'

'Where do you live, Mister May.' He looks again at my lacy nightdress. 'I suppose it is *Mister* May?'

I smile ingratiatingly at him, which makes him take a step backwards, stepping neatly into a pile of doggy leavings on the footpath.

'All right, then. Whose clothes are those? Where do you live? What's your game?'

'Lobelia Dugfondle. Eighty-four, Copper Bottom, and darts. But not necessarily in that order.'

He takes all this down in his book.

'Oh ho. So you're Mrs. Dugfondle's latest . . . I see. And I hear she's gone off on some jaunt.'

'To the West Indies, but not Jamaica and not Bahamas. She'll be back in a month.' I gabble frantically, wanting to get this humiliating episode over. And in any case I am bursting for a pee. Not a new pee, but the same old pee.

'And you thought you'd put on her scanties and parade up and down through a decent village to the confusion of the subjects of Her Majesty the Queen and the general affrightment of horses, contrary to the...'

'Yes. I mean: No! I was down at the launderette and it went wrong and all my clothes got wet and not dry like these and with...'

A gust of wind flutters at my garment, and it blows up around my thighs. If it had blown up the Houses of Parliament the reaction would hardly have been greater.

He points at poor Edgar, and reaches for his truncheon. 'Lor love us! Have you got a licence for that? And don't wave it at me. It might go off.'

I grin and try and cover my dignity, but the feathers seem to be shedding.

'How did you get it that...? I mean I've tried weights hanging on the...' He remembers who he is and where he is and what he's supposed to be doing.

'I suppose I ought to believe you, as nobody but a raving loony would have got himself in this position. Now cut along home before Mrs. Vatman comes out and loses her self-control. Go on.'

I have convinced him of my innocence!

'I reckoned you might have been the phantom knicker-nicker that's been going round Withering Bumple,' says the sturdy officer, the idea lodging in his brain.

'Not me, sir. Knickers. Wouldn't touch them.'

At which moment, the bottom falls out of the shopping-bag and out of my world and the pavement is flooded with a stunning and brightly-coloured array of Lobelia's underwear.

There follows a somewhat long exchange and mart of words, but at last he is satisfied that I am innocent. But it is a long and uphill struggle.

'One more suspicious word out of you about ladies' clothes my lad and your feet won't touch the ground. Now go and put on a pair of your own cavalry twills.'

Backing away, I wave a cheerful hand. 'Right. Actually, I don't wear that sort of trousers. I always wear jeans.'

It takes me half an hour to persuade the station sergeant that I mean well. And that I mean jeans as in blue trousers and not as in Jeannie with the light brown hair.

It is not my day.

But nothing worse can happen.

And they do run me home in a car, still wearing the frilly nightie.

Push me out of the vehicle, having first found out that the launderette is locked up for the day, with my clothes still in it.

'Any more trouble from you, Mister May, and you will find yourself charged with committing a nuisance. And failing that, I know a fellow not far from here who'd really fancy you in that nightdress.'

I wave him a friendly Harvey as he drives away, making sure he can't actually see it, and walk wearily up the path of eighty-four, noting the twitching curtains of Mrs. Vatman, who will get free coffee from her friends for months on the strength of this.

I don't care. Nothing else is going wrong today. I feel it in my bones.

Stupid bones!

I reach the door and my hand goes to my pocket for the key.

Which *is* in my pocket.

Of my best strides, safely locked away in the launderette!

Stupid bones!

Don't worry about the window-cleaner bit not being here. It's in the next chapter. Honest!

CHAPTER EIGHT

Not that I want you to get the impression that all members of the May family are stupid. Anyway, anyone could forget a key.

(Publisher's Note: But not when naked except for a lady's flimsy night garment.)

I shall treat that with the contempt it deserves.

No. My Uncle Nick is quite a sharp bird at times. My old man is also something of a sage. Really knows his onions.

My Uncle Nick goes to this sauna bath and massage parlour. Nudge, nudge, know what I mean? Massage, massage, they go. They go, and you come.

First time he's been to one of them, and he walks into this cubicle and strips off. In comes a tall blonde bird with knockers on her like twin warheads. Wearing a short overall, which is not quite over all.

Throws him a dirty scrap of towel, and produces a bottle of cooking oil. Doesn't say anything, but just starts to rub this smelly grease into him, humming to herself, and still smoking a cigarette, pausing every now and again to exchange boring conversation with her friend in the next cubicle.

Uncle Nick is not happy with this, and manages to roll over on his back, his flagpole raising the scrap of towel in the air. The masseuse ignores it, apart from giving it a bang with the edge of her hand that nearly ruins the chances of Uncle N. having any more little Nicks.

He mentions the naughty subject of why he's come there, and she finally puts on a pair of rubber gloves covered in grease marks, and gives him a touch of the five-fingered widow.

After it's over, Uncle Nick calls the girl back, she being half-way through the door ready for her tea-break, and he gives her a five pound tip. Then walks quickly out, leaving her flabber exceedingly well gasted.

Goes back a week later, and asks for the same girl. When she sees him, she makes an excuse, and rushes off, coming back after five minutes looking immaculate. Clean white robe, deliberately pulled apart to show that she is a cat-lover and believes in giving her pussy plenty of fresh air.

Uncle Nick gets spotless towels wrapped around him, and scented oil at three quid an ounce. Massages him in places where he doesn't even know he has places. Up goes the flag-pole, and she giggles and pulls off the towel, and relieves the situation in – according to Uncle Nick – four different ways in thirty-five minutes. Goes with him in the shower and comes with him in the shower.

After she's dried him all over, she kisses him goodbye, then helps him to get dressed and kisses him goodbye on the lips.

Waits for her tip.

Uncle Nick grins at her and presses a five pence piece into her hot little hand.

'What the hell's this for?' she screams. 'It was a fiver last time, and you didn't get nothing like you did this time.'

'Quite right,' says wise old Uncle Nick.

'Well?'

'Well. You see my dear young girl, the five pence tip was for *last* time. The five pound tip was for *this* time.'

Might not be funny, but at least it's a moral tale. Most of them are immoral tales.

In case you prefer the immoral ones, here's a very quick quickie.

What's the difference between a classy brothel, and a circus?

Give up?

At the circus you see a lot of cunning stunts.

I am reclining in a bath filled to the brim with hot, soapy water, and some lovely smelly oil. I love oil in a bath. Oil be loving you. . .

The kids are at school, and Charity is off to work, with a clean pair of knickers on. I know because she shows them to me every morning without fail. The breakfast is smouldering in the bin, and there is a mountain of housework to be done.

I don't know how women manage to fit it in. Dolly has been shifted to another round, after complaints from some of the customers about her habit of having a quick fill-up of something or other (mainly the other) from me in the middle of her work. Mrs. Vatman I suspect.

But last night I pay her back for it.

There is a field at the back of our row of houses, and there are some cows there during the day who seem to exist on a diet of bovine laxative. The world drops out of their bottoms every couple of minutes.

I sneak out at dusk and get a bucket and fill it up with Guernsey poo-poo. After dark, I creep over to Mrs. Vatman's front path, with the bucket, and a pile of newspaper and a box of matches. I'm not worried about being spotted, as the whole of Copper Bottom will be glued to their tellies, watching the nine hundred and eighty-seventh episode of *Crossroads*. A show that I will not join in the knocking of. Folks deserve the television they watch, and they watch the television they deserve.

Work that one out.

I reach her front door, and get things ready for the big revenge. I'll teach her to stop me fitting it in first thing each morning.

Carefully roll the papers into a funnel-shaped parcel. Fill it with the cow-pat-a-cake. Still, very liquid. Place it on the step. Set fire to a corner of the dry outside paper, and ring the bell.

Leap faster than a speeding bullet back to the shadows of eighty-four's front porch.

Watch.

Out comes Mrs. Vatman, face curled up into a snarl at being

interrupted at one of the nine hundred and eighty-seven key moments. Sees the smoking paper.

And here's the beauty of it all.

Mrs. V. thinks it's just a pile of smoking paper. So she jumps up and down on it in her best pink fluffy slippers to put it out!

Like the comics say: 'Splat!!!!!!'

That was just to explain that Jonny and Edgar have not been getting much fun these last few days. Still, Lobelia is home in a very few weeks, and I reckon I can hold out, or hold on, for that long.

But I lie in my bath, not bothering to pull the curtains as nobody can see in unless they're on a ladder, and close my eyes, wishing that my fairy godmother would provide me with a lovely lady.

Talking of fairies, did I ever mention the gay fireman who was always sliding down Poles? I didn't? Then I won't.

I stand up to wash my most intimate details, giving the credentials a swift one-two with the flannel, I am conscious of a draught from the partly-open window behind me. Like the wind that whistles for ever up the Khyber Pass.

By Chilly and Winds! There *is* an odd whistling noise.

'Nothing like putting a brave face to the world, is there dear?'

I try and turn round, sit down, climb out of the bath, reach for the towel and faint all at the same time. My foot slips on a sliver of Pears' best transparent, and I go bum over brainbox in the water.

There is a deal of wallowing and swallowing.

'Here. I haven't seen anything like that since the last time *Moby Dick* was on telly.'

I am beginning not to like this voice. Coming out of space like that, frightening a body out of its skin. And it was only in its skin to begin with. It doesn't surprise me, as the voice is all high and effeminate, like a teenage girl.

I manage to get my head out of the water and wipe my face dry, ready to give this nosy git with the silly voice a piece of my mind.

'Oh.' Not to mention 'Oooh!'

I see instantly why the bloke has got such a high voice, like a teenage girl.

All together now: Because it *is* a teenage girl! And a very pretty one at that. Leaning halfway through the bathroom window, grinning at me, waving a bit of soggy chamois leather.

The shock of seeing this is even greater than the shock of hearing a voice and my feet go again as I try and bend down to lock away my testimonials behind the flannel. I slip over, and my toe, by some freak of nature, becomes wedged in the cold tap. If I try and sit up, I slide back again, and I find myself jammed tighter than a Scotsman's wallet.

'Having trouble, love?' comes a somewhat unsympathetic cry from the window.

'Just go away, and leave me alone, or I'll have the law on you. Creeping up at the windows of a respectable houseman like that.'

'You want me to go away?'

'Yes. I don't know what you're doing here in the first place.'

'Cleaning your windows, darling, but if you want me to shove off, I'll go now.'

And the face vanishes from the bathroom window.

I review the situation a whole lot faster than Fagin in *Oliver*.

'Window cleaner?'

The voice is at the bottom of the ladder. 'Yes. You can pay my uncle next time. I'm just filling in for him. Byee!'

That got rid of her.

All I have to do now is get out of the bath, and...

Get out of the bath.

Help.

'Help!'

'What's wrong?' Thank my lucky stars. And anybody else you care to name. She hasn't gone away.

'Could you, sort of like, as it were, maybe come back here for a minute?'

'What?'

'Please!'

'All right.' The clatter of a ladder being shoved up against the wall, and the head appears again. I notice this time that it is a blonde head, with sensuous Mick Jagger lips and bright blue eyes.

The blue eyes look inquiringly at me.

'I sort of seem to be a little stuck.'

'Hello, little stuck. What do you want?'

'As I slipped in the bath, my toe's got jammed up the cold tap and I just can't move it.'

'What am I supposed to do, love? I get paid for cleaning windows, not removing toes from taps.'

What a mercenary bitch! Here I am, a suffering human being, and all she can think about is money.

'I'll pay you a fiver.'

Well, the water is getting colder, and the kids'll be back from school in an hour, and the front door is locked and all that. It just means the supermarket'll have to go short for a few days.

Her bright eyes brighten even more at the mention of the word 'fiver', and she sticks her head further through the window. I find this all very embarrassing, and cover my shrinking dignity with the flannel.

It's a *big* flannel, that's how!

'Is the door open, or do you want me to come in through the window?'

'A gentleman is more concerned about *when* a lady comes rather than how. Just come through the window.'

With an effort she manages to squeeze through the gap, and I can see what my rescuer looks like.

And the looks I like.

If it wasn't so humiliating to be stuck here flat on my back, with Edgar only just keeping his head above water, I might fancy my chances here.

'You're looking at me as though you fancy your chances. Proper little male chauvinist piglet, aren't you?'

'No. Not at all. If I was I wouldn't be running a house while the lady of it is swanning around the West Indies for six weeks.'

'Jamaica?'

I am not in the mood for that one again, so I simply shake my head. The lady is not unattractive.

The blonde head is on top of a figure that my practised eye estimates at being a nice even forty-twenty-forty.

She's wearing a blue denim blouse with a blue denim jacket and a pair of snug-fitting blue denim trousers. Her shoes are also blue, but not made of denim. As far as I can see from my lowly position.

'Now then, let's see what we can do.'

I clutch the flannel to the family jewels, but she is very business-like, and bends over, tugging at the offending little limb. I give what sounds to me a convincing impression of a pig being slaughtered, and she lets go, looking at me with a mixture of sympathy and humour.

'Trouble is, I can't get at the right angle to pull it out properly.'

I have had the same trouble myself at odd times. Some very odd times.

She sits down on the loo, in lieu of anywhere else to sit, being careful to put the back down first. Seeing her there, looking at me with her head on one side, gets Edgar working well, and to my blushing shame, he begins to lift the flannel in the air like Billy Smart's big top on the way up.

'Hey. You need a bigger flannel, don't you?' she grins, and

I grin back, feeling less embarrassed, and a lot more randy.

'Shouldn't we introduce ourselves, seeing as how we're all together like this?'

'You may be in the altogether, lover, but I'm certainly not.' There is a significant pause. 'Not yet, anyway.'

'Well, my name is Jonny May, and I will be very grateful if you get me out of this.'

'My name's Penny Spender, and if you so much as grin at that name I shall jam something beside your toe up that tap.'

We both grin again at the idea. I grin and nearly bare it, but a last-second grab at the flannel keeps the basic details under cover.

'These are new trousers I bought for this job, and then I find they shrink if they get wet. Lot of use for a window-cleaner, isn't it?'

She takes off her shoes, and looks at the bath of steaming water. I suddenly guess that she is considering pulling the plug on me, leaving me as waterless as a duck's back.

'No. Penny, please. Cold porcelain is a very chilling prospect.'

'Well . . . the only alternative will be if I take off my trousers, 'cos I can't help unless I get in there with you.'

'I'll do anything. . .'

'It's not what you might do, it's stopping you doing it that I'm worried about.'

I try to look as innocent as a new-born babe. 'Well, I'm certainly not going to leap up and rape you from this position, am I?'

I forget that she is a liberated lady.

'Think it's funny, do you?'

'No! Not at all.'

'Lucky for you. It's not a lot of fun for a woman, being flat on her back, all helpless, while some great. . .'

She stops talking, and a gleam comes into her eye, as though an idea has leaped into her mind. I cannot imagine what it can be, but lying here, flat on my back, all helpless while she. . . Oh, no! Thank you, but: No!!

'Well, well, well. Wait till I get to the next meeting of Double-L.'

'Double-L?' I ask, with a sinking heart, and it isn't just the water turning cold.

'Liberated Lady. I'm the chair-person this month. We've got a branch in the local town. And here I am with a real live pink pig, all helpless and ready to go.'

'You'll never make me ready to come,' I joke bravely, trying to remember how E. Flynn Esq. used to look facing the firing squad.

'Wait till I tell them about this. You did say that you'd do anything to get free of that tap, didn't you?'

'No.'

She begins to put her shoes back on again and climb out through the window.

'Yes. Anything. But not that.'

'Don't you fancy me, Jonny? It is Jonny, isn't it, my little lover?'

'Yes it is, and not so much of the little either.'

'Tut, tut. Penis-pride, I suppose.'

I blush at such a filthy word coming from a lady's lips. It reminds me of the time that a very respectable lady of my acquaintance tells me how she went as a gal to the Boat Race and was so excited at the end that she kissed the cox of both crews.

'Look. I'm hardly in a position to stop you doing more or less what you want, but I promise you that I shall do nothing to help you, and I shall take no pleasure in it.'

'That's what they all say, but we'll see, shall we, Jonny?'

She peels off her top clothes, followed in no time flat by her bottom clothes. Her top half is at no time flat, and she lives up to the liberated image by not containing her spam swingers in anything but air. Edgar can hardly contain himself, and I can hardly contain Edgar. Penny looks down and laughs, setting her cream jellies a'wobble.

'You might not reckon to get any pleasure out of it, but *that* is lapping it up already.'

I can't deny it. I mean, it sticks out a mile.

(Publisher's Note: I'm sure I hardly need to reassure those concerned ladies that this is just Mister May indulging his usual flair for exaggeration.)

He stayed too long at the flair, did that one.

By now Penny is wearing only a bright smile, and a pair of teeny-weeny manhole covers. She whips them off with all the ease of an experienced paint-stripper, and dangles them in one hand, looking down at me.

'Come on in, the water's fine,' I joke.

'I can't get in and help you with *that* poking up like something out of a U-Boat film. Can't you do something with it?'

'I was hoping that you might be able to help.'

She pauses with one toe in the water, just alongside my left hip. 'Wait a minute, sonny. I'm the one doing you a favour, and anything else that happens is a bonus. For me and not for you. Is that clear?'

She prods me with her toe, neatly tweaking the flannel off poor Edgar, who seems to glory in his exposure. I close my eyes and think of Tina Turner.

By the time I open my mincies, Penny is spending her time with me. She is in the bath, and has straddled me, facing towards the taps. Being a gentleman, I feel that I ought not to give too much detail of what is happening. The lady has to bend down to reach my toe, which brings her . . . the very top of her thighs, within seven hundredths of an inch of my nose and mouth.

I'm only human, despite what my publisher tries to get you to believe. My mother always tells me how rude it is to stick out my tongue.

What do you know? She's right. It is *very* rude, and it provokes something halfway between a giggle and a scream from Penny, who jumps, and slips backwards, so that my tongue becomes inextricably linked to her spice-box.

'Not bad,' she grunts, still working away at my other end, pulling and wriggling like mad, which makes what is happening at my end even more interesting. 'I was always told that the ideal lover was a Frenchman with a nine inch tongue who could breathe through his ears. Now I believe . . . Oooooh . . . believe it.'

I lack the ability to breathe through my ears so I am getting a bit short of oxygen. And I am getting a crick in the neck. Better than a cricklewood. Or a cricklewouldn't.

To stop herself slipping any further, in which case I would, in my own way, be rivalling Miss Lovelace, Penny grabs hold of Edgar with one hand. He has been untouched by human hand for a long time – by female human hand, that is – and shows his lack of breeding by straining to even greater heights.

Trying to aid my tongue, which is finding it hard going (actually it is Edgar who is finding it hard going. My tongue couldn't have it softer and sweeter) I reach up and under and through and in with my own fingers.

Penny doesn't seem to notice and keeps her hips pressing back in my direction, working up a nice fast rhythm. Slowly her bottom slides lower down, so that I have to reach forward a long way to keep my light-fingered infantry pressing home their charge. The way she is going down on me (?) she will soon find that Edgar is going to . . . very soon . . . nearly . . . in a couple of. . .

'Oh!'

'Oh!'

One of those is Penny and the other one is me. It doesn't make any difference who says it first. Happy to be in his favourite playroom, Edgar begins to make a fearful exhibition of himself, leaping about all over the place. Up and down and side to side.

Bathwater is splashing over the edge of the bath, all over the fur rug. Well, Lobelia shouldn't have put a fur rug in a bathroom. Out of place. Like a raised toilet seat in a convent.

I find myself sitting up, pressing my chest against Penny's silken back, both hands full of . . . you know. Just both hands full.

It must be at about this moment that my toe slips out of the tap, but we are both rather too busy to notice it go.

The velvet vacuum cleaner is going full force. I don't know whether climbing up ladders helps develop certain muscles, but Penny has some very well-developed muscles. The water gets like the Atlantic in a force nine gale, but both of us are past caring.

Having it away in the bath is not actually something I'd recommend as a habit, but it's an exciting change. I don't even notice the hammering my back is taking, nor the fact that her knees are wearing grooves in my thighs as she rises and falls.

By reaching all the way round her, my nimble right hand can manage a bit of extra massage on her booster button. This does the trick and we both splash through the finishing-line. As she breasts the tape (?), she gives out with a scream that I fear might shatter the windows. It gives my ears a pane, anyway.

And she promptly collapses backwards, thrusting me right under water, lying on top of me, while I flail away like a drowning kitten. Penny is a big girl, and I wonder for a few moments, if this is the end of Jonny.

(Publisher's Note: I should be so lucky!)

But she eventually rises, and stands astride me, giving me a wonderful chance to admire her references at very close quarters.

'Is there any more hot water, Jonny?' she asks, smiling down at me, and giving a happy Edgar a nice gentle touch with her foot.

'Yes. Probably. Why?'

'Seems a shame to waste the chance of a real bath, after all that exercise. Then maybe you could show me the rest of the house.'

'Why not?'

'Specially the bedroom.'

If cleanliness is truly next to Godliness, then Penny and I become one of the most Godly couples in the whole of Withering Bumple.

I wash her plump little bath buns for her, and she reciprocates for me. And if you haven't had a naked girl reciprocate for you, then you haven't lived, my friends.

It is nearly two hours later that Penny finally takes her leave. She takes my fiver as well, which is fair enough, though being a liberated lady she goes to a lot of trouble to point out that she is taking it for freeing my toe and not for anything else.

'I'm no sponger,' she explains.

'Could have fooled me,' say I, pointing to the steamy bathroom.

We have a bit of a giggle, and a fumble, but she has other windows to clean, and for me. . . ? Well, you know that a man's work is never done.

Penny kisses me goodbye. As she is only doing this for a week, I doubt we shall ever meet again. But she has given me a new experience and I'm grateful for that. I wave her a goodbye and she vanishes into the mist carrying her ladder.

There's something about ships that pass in the night. I turn back to eighty-four, feeling both better and worse. Better because it was one of the finest hours since the Battle of Britain. Worse because I am getting fed up with doing this housework. Same old thing; week in and week out. Very boring it is.

Once Lobelia returns from her holiday the only steps that I shall be taking will be long ones. That's if I can keep away from Charity and save myself from those blunt scissors. To find out if I can, just keep reading.

Haven't had a good Brummie joke for some time. Here's one I like. This Brummie is leaning up against this high wall, when an old brass sidles up to him. 'Want a bunk-up, dearie?' she asks him.

'Why?' he says. 'What's on the other side?'

CHAPTER NINE

Rummaging upstairs through Lobelia's drawers one wet afternoon – well, it's the only pleasure left to me – I come across a parcel of letters and things that her late husband must have left when he slipped away to a better place.

Not that I've met many better places than Lobelia's; and so cleverly concealed..

Among them is a short poem, that gives me a sad insight into what the latter years of his marriage must have been like. It tells of the decline and fall of his sitting member. That became a lying member as years advanced.

It goes like this:

'With sad regret I now remember,
Those happy days of youth and fun.
When all my limbs were soft and tender;
Did I say all? Well, all but one.
Those happy days are gone for ever,
Those joyous times of naughty fun,
Now all my limbs are hard and stiff;
Did I say all? Well, all but one.'

There is a highlight coming up in my life. Like finding dog-crap in the pavement. That sort of highlight.

Faith and Bobby are thirteen, which may be unlucky for some. October 29th, which I find from a bit of research is a date they share mainly with Doctor Goebbels. He who, from the song my old man used to sing in the bath, had none at all.

The twins are looking forward with great excitement to this happy day. Bobby and I have an exchange of views in which he asks for a party for them, with a conjuror, this being the latest status symbol among the brats of Withering Bumple, which is a fine status of affairs.

'No.'

'I said please, didn't I?' Bobby has been amazingly better behaved since I give him the order of the belt.

'Yes, but no. No. That's my very last word on the subject so forget it.'

As he goes out he mumbles something just loud enough for me to *nearly* hear it.

'What?'

'Just said that I reckon it's my family duty to tell Mum when she gets back all about you and Charity.'

'What about Charity and me?' My voice goes higher than the bill for Concorde.

'The may me and Faith keep seeing you looking up her skirt at her knickers. And she keeps pushing up against you when she's got nothing on at all. And. . .'

I have a strange vision of a pair of blunt scissors, cutting short my prospects. But to give a party for these two, and their frightful companions! That really is too much to expect.

'Unusual party, Mister May. Most unusual. Where did you get the ideas from?'

The Jonathan May Book of Natural Disasters, is the answer to that one.

I manage to wring the minimal concession from them that there will be not more than twelve children in all, and they stick to that. But the other ten teeny monsters all seem to have the looks of a church choir and the manners of the Incredible Hulk.

The lady who is impressed with my arrangements, and who is also thoroughly newted, lives down the posh end of Copper Bottom, and is a pillar of the church. From what I hear about her and the vicar, that should be pillow of the church. A lovely lady in her early thirties, who has inherited three children in their early teens from a second husband who is heading for an early grave.

Her name is Seraphina Blanco. Maiden name was Bloggs, so I'm not sure if she's better off or not. Now I wouldn't want it put about that Seraphina is stupid, but she goes to the local doctor, complaining about stabbing pains in her eyes every time she drinks a cup of tea. After a lot of research, he locates the source of the trouble. Tells her to remember to take the spoon out next time.

You probably want to know what she means by the party being unusual. I don't give a flying trapeze if you do or not, because you're going to anyway. Seraphina, like the other mums in the village, brings her little Mary Jane along to the party promptly at three. But unlike the other mums, she stays.

Charity has gone off to a free concert at Hyde Park, featuring Warsun, Foolsgold and Central Heating. Three up and coming groups who I suspect will eventually be down and going.

The unusual party bit?

It's partly the food I've arranged.

I just don't understand what went wrong with the sponge cake, but when I cut into it, instead of being firm and fluffy, it runs all over the plate in a liquid stream. And I know that I should have remembered to put the ice cream in the freezer as soon as I get back from the shops, but there are so many things to do, and so little time in which to do them.

That sounds almost like a famous quote. Not quite a quote, though.

And the fruit salad isn't exactly *salad*, because that tends to mean more than one kind of fruit. Well, guavas are very nice, and when you've bought a special offer of forty-seven tins, then you have to use them up somehow. These are times of economy, as Mrs. Thatcher is always telling us. Trouble is with a lot of politicians, the only economising they do is on brain-power.

I know one M.P. who used to think that a draughtsman was someone who opened and closed windows!

When the little dear ones see this huge bowl filled with this odd fruit, they all start making vomiting noises. Faith holds her nose and cries out: 'Blimey! I think somebody's already eaten these once.'

I reassure them, and tell them that they are merely something exotic from abroad, called guavas.

'I thought that was what bats left behind,' pipes up Bobby.

I smile and flick him hard just behind the right ear as I go by, which effectively silences him. Trouble is, now he mentions it, I think that they might be something that bats leave behind as well.

The bread and butter is fine. I can't do it. I can't lie to you. I spent so much on the special offer on the guano – I mean guavas – that I couldn't afford the bread and butter.

But the beans go down well.

Down the garbage disposer well.

What about the fry-up?

Burned-up.

And I seem to have run out of saucepans and pots again. That's three times in the last four weeks. Don't make them like they used to.

Still; Lobelia is due back in less than a fortnight, and then things will be fine and dandy. Or fine and beano if that's your fancy. Personally, I'm a wizard, rover, hotspur, adventure man myself. I identify with the incredible Wilson, who can do an amazing number of things in such a small amount of time. I can do a small number of things in an amazing amount of time!

So there isn't a lot of food to go round. But some of the children have brought bottles of what they call 'fruit punch' which speedily makes them very happy. I sample a sip, and the only fruit tree it's been near is the vodka tree or the whiskey bush.

I also go in the toilet for a momentary flush of quiet, and one of the girls from down the other end of the village comes giggling out, giving me a warm, wet kiss on the mouth as she does. When I go in I am sure that I can smell some exotic herbal smell. Doubtless one of them has brought some sort of menthol cigarettes or other.

Whatever it does, they all seem to be in a high good humour, though the games that I have prepared for them are sadly neglected.

The donkey hangs limply on the wall, totally tail-less, though someone has given him an extra appendage which nature had never intended.

The girl from the loo lurches up to me, and tugs me by the collar. Feeling the eyes of Mrs. Blanco boring at my back – well, she is a very boring person – I push her gently away, careful that my hands don't wander over her youthful pastures.

'Listen, Jonny,' she whispers, breaking up again into fits of giggling, that shake all of her body. Can she really only be twelve? 'Got a riddle for you.'

'What is it?'

'What's the difference between a vitamin and a hormone? Come on.'

'I don't know, Jenny, what is the difference between a vitamin and a hormone?'

Not that I care.

Her face spreads its smile wider than the Severn Bridge. 'You can't hear a vitamin.' And she wanders off, swaying her hips to some new ballad about a chicken having its neck wrung by a blind man. Very popular with the tweenies, I'm told.

You can't hear a vitamin. Don't get it. Oh, yes I do. Whore moan. Very good.

I mean, disgraceful!

There seems to be a squabble over Scrabble in the living-room. I am delighted when a couple of the boys ask if we've got a set in the house. I pop in the living-room a few minutes ago, and have to put a stop to some high jinx. And I do not mean Chinese tight-rope walkers.

Mrs. Vatman has brought round her adorable little boy – John Thomas Vatman, and he has been playing with Mrs. Blanco's little girl. The aforementioned Mary Jane. Mr. Vatman has just brought round a clean hanky for his son, and before I know what's happening, he and Seraphina are having the most peculiar conversation.

'You and your John Thomas!' is the first thing I hear from an obviously enraged Mrs. Blanco.

'I don't think much of your Mary Jane, either.' Well said, Bwana Vatman. Neither do I.

'Well! Now I've heard everything. I go in that room, and what do I see?'

'It's only a game, Mrs. Blanco.'

'Game!!!!!' The volume control is set higher than a Concorde take-off. 'Call that a game!!!'

'Kids playing.'

'I am not having your John Thomas playing that sort of game with my little Mary Jane.'

'My John Thomas is not in the least interested in your Mary Jane.'

Fifteen-all.

Mrs. Blanco to serve.

'You could have mooled fee.'

Fault.

Second service.

'You could have fooled me. That great thing standing up there, threatening Mary Jane.'

'Your Mary Jane is bigger than my John Thomas. And if there's any threatening going on, then it was Mary Jane that was threatening John Thomas.'

This whole conversation has a nasty touch of the Lady Chatterleys.

'I know what your John Thomas needs, and if I get my hands on him, then he'll get what for.'

What four is she talking about? Four Preps? Four Freshmen? Four he's a jolly good fellow?

'I'd like to get your Mary Jane over me knee and give her a damned good licking.'

I know that my publisher is getting worried over this passage of dialogue, but I can't for the life of me see why. Can you? I mean, it's just a couple of neighbours having a bit of a row about their children.

Isn't it?

(Publisher's Note: Is it?)

Course it is.

Coarse it is.

'If you try and lick my Mary Jane, then I shall give your John Thomas a swift kick.'

Can have nasty effects that. Like the time my old mum put some Comfort in my old man's bath. And everything went soft and springy.

Personally, I am in favour (of the month) of letting his John Thomas and her Mary Jane just get together and see what happens. I come in like Doctor Kissinger and pour water over the troubled oil.

Incidentally, did you know that the in-thing at American parties is to take it in turns to do an impression of the amiable Doctor? Every now and then someone will cry out: 'I wonder who's Kissinger now.'

I persuade John Thomas and Mary Jane to kiss and make up, which they finally do, watched by their smirking parents. Mr. Vatman shoves off, and Mrs. Blanco carries on drinking. Starring Sid James, Bernard Bresslaw, Barbara Windsor and Kenneth Williams.

The food has nearly all gone – most of it on the floor and

ceiling. The drink has also been drained. The children are getting restless, but Jonny is about to pull his master-stroke.

'Children. Kiddies!! Quiet please!!' At last a bit of hush descends. 'I have a nice surprise for you all now.'

'Good. He's goin' to cut his bleedin' throat,' croaks an unidentified voice from near the back of the room.

'No. I have a magician for you.'

I've heard louder applause in a chapel of rest.

'His name is Uncle Rupert and here he is.'

I wave my hand in the direction of the kitchen, where I last saw the jolly figure of the conjuror.

Nothing.

'Ha, ha.' I laugh with all the merriment of a marooned sailor. 'They say conjurors love to deceive us, and this appearance is certainly deceptive.'

That joke goes down as well as a Liverpool supporter at an Everton game.

'Just got see about. . .' I let my voice fade away to nothing and speed into the kitchen, leaving the merry Mrs. Blanco propped up against the wall, trying to hold back the hordes.

She reminds me about the woman who goes in the butcher's and asks for some bacon, and says: 'Will you make it lean?'

'Certainly, madam,' replies the butcher. 'Which way do you want it to lean?'

There's also a jest about a fishmonger, but maybe I'll leave that to the end of the chapter.

Things are not well in the Dugfondle kitchen. If Lobelia were to walk in now, I fear that she would reach for the blunt scissors without even bothering to find out how I and Charity have been having it off. I mean, getting on.

Uncle Rupert is somewhat the worse for wear. Wear's Imperial Whiskey. There is a bottle in one of the cupboards that I have brought in for purely medicinal reasons, and it is now rolling on its side, with a quarter inch of amber liquid sloshing around in it.

Also lying on his side, with several inches of the amber liquid sloshing around in his innards, is the above-mentioned Uncle Rupert. Wearing a silly grin and a false nose.

' 'Lo, ole man. Just slip me the word when you're ready for me to stuff my poo on . . . I mean do my stuff for the li'le bleeders in there. Ole Uncle Rupert won't let you down. Cerumbs no.'

It is bad enough to see my entertainer in this state, but to find him talking like a refugee from Just William somehow makes it worse.

Madame Blanco comes unexpectedly (don't we all?) into the kitchen, and recoils like a broken spring when she sees the nasty mess on the floor.

'Is that . . . ?' she asks, pointing a finger at poor Uncle Rupert.

'Yes,' say I, glancing interestedly at the floor to see if there are yet any signs of it opening up and swallowing me out of sight. No such luck.

'You've got to do something,' hisses Mrs. Blanco like a punctured inner tube. 'They'll riot in there if they find out there's no conjuror.'

I have hastily drained the contents of the rolling bottle, which mixes interestingly with the three glasses of fruit punch, giving a warm glow that even spreads to Edgar.

'Riot on, sister,' I say, giggling at my own brand of wit. 'Don't worry, Seraphina, my little flower, Jonny will pull something out.'

From the look of interest she casts at my mid-section, I rapidly suss out that Mrs. Blanco would not be averse in a poem . . . averse to a spot of the piston and cylinder game.

There is a groaning noise from the floor. Uncle Rupert is looking a little wan. On second thoughts, he is looking a big one.

The noise is escalating faster than my old man's drink bill.

Something has to be done. The only question that has to be answered is WHAT???

I stick my head round the door, narrowly missing being clobbered by a well-aimed chunk of guava, and call Bobby and Faith in the hall. They both seem flushed and unusually giggly, and the aroma of those herbal cigarettes hangs heavy in the air.

'What do you want? We're just having fun in there. Starting to go with a swing.'

'I . . . I wondered if you wanted to play any quiet games, instead of being quite so noisy?'

'Games!' Faith pulls a face like Charles Laughton in the *Hunchback of Notre Damebusters*.

'Yes. Like "Pass the Parcel" and "Musical Chairs" and "Postman's Knock.'"

'What about your conjuror?' asks Bobby.

'He's . . . not very well.'

'Yeah. Pissed, inn'e? Like the gay dwarf whose friends were always coming over a little queer.'

I don't know where they learn them all, but it certainly isn't from me.

'No. No he isn't. Well, actually, yes he is, but don't tell anyone. The last time I saw him he'd crawled out into the garden shed to sleep it off.'

'Wouldn't dream of mentioning it, Jonny. And I reckon those games you mentioned sound as though they might be a lot of fun.'

'What?' exclaims Faith, looking at her twin brother as though he's lost his marbles.

Which reminds me of the time my brother Morrie takes some ball-bearings to school to play marbles with. Accidentally drops them in the classroom and they roll all over the place. Teacher sees them and calls out, without thinking: 'Who has steel balls?'

Quick as a flash, Morrie shouts out: 'Superman!'

Bobby nudges his sister, and turns on me a smile of pure innocent hatred. 'Just as long as you and any other adults promise to stay out of the way.'

'Well . . .'

'And we'll promise that you won't have any damage, and hardly any noise. It is a deal?'

By now it sounds as though they are filming a remake of *Zulu* in the living-room, so I weakly nod. Sometimes I nod twice-weekly. They vanish back through the door, and the noise ceases like turning off a hose. I hear mumbling, and then a cheer, quickly muffled.

I go back in the kitchen, where Seraphina is leaning up the wall, absently scratching her thigh, skirt up round her hips. There is a lop-sided smile hanging grimly on the corners of her lips, and it doesn't take a Maigret, or a migraine, to spot she is *very* well-newted.

There isn't much else to do for an hour or so, and we quickly find we are well-newted to each other.

Since the kitchen is adjacent, and since there is a small serving-hatch in the wall with the living-room, I decide that it is a part of my duty to keep an eye on the activities of the little children entrusted to my care.

(Publisher's Note: He means that he enjoys being a Peeping Tom!)

He's got a nerve! A big building behind his trendy hovel has just been turned into a nurses' home, and my publisher all of a sudden gets interested in astronomy and buys a great big telescope. Sort of like a Peeping Tom in Cinerama.

I ease up the hatch about half an inch so that I can see in without being seen. And what a scene!

The games that I suggest to them are, as you will obviously remember, 'Pass the Parcel', 'Musical Chairs' and 'Postman's Knock'.

Have you ever seen 'Strip Pass The Parcel'? Then you haven't lived. None of these kids are over fifteen. When I was that age we boys all hung around and argued whether Biggles was a better pilot than Braddock. And any girl who tried to spy on us was likely to get her dress lifted while we all smirked at her sensible woollen blue bloomers.

In fact, there is still some similarity. Much of this game consists of lifting girl's dresses, but somehow things are different. Girls of that age weren't quite as well developed then as they are now. And they didn't wear such tight, satin knickers in such interesting colours.

As the music stops they all tear at the parcel, and when it starts again the one who had the parcel has to take off an article of clothing. I feel hot breath in my ear, and Seraphina is kneeling at my side, eyes also glued to the narrow slit of the hatch. She is breathing heavily, and I put my hand round her shoulders to steady her.

Honest.

Several of the boys are down to their trousers, and at least one of the young ladies is wearing only her knickers and what I suppose passes for a bra, though it seems to have been made from a gerbil's jockstrap.

Seraphina is coming in short pants. Sorry. Slip of the pen there. Her breath is coming in short pants. And I feel that things have gone far enough.

For the time being.

So I load up a tray with cokes and burst into this scene of juvenile debauchery, crying: 'Anyone for anything long and cool?'

Jenny sidles up to me, adjusting her gusset, and whispers in my ear: 'I'd like something long and hot, and I bet you've got just what I need.'

I disentangle her fingers from the heirlooms, wait until they are all more or less dressed, and then walk out, suggesting that 'Musical Chairs' might be a nicer game for them to play.

Why do they agree so readily?

Back to the kitchen, where I put my eye back to the slit. Of the hatch, I keep telling you.

'Musical Chairs'!!

Huh!

Every time the music stops, then you're all supposed to make a dive for the chairs, and the one who fails has to stand out. Take away a chair, and then start again, until only one's left.

That's how we used to play it.

Not here.

Not with the Dugfondles' devils' brood.

The boys sit there instead of chairs. The girls have to try and sit on their laps. The one left out then goes and sits in the corner, with the boy who has also moved out. They seem to be carrying out some form of tonsil-exploration, using only their tongues. Perhaps all that sitting and rolling around has hurt them, as they also appear to be rubbing each other better.

Mrs. Blanco takes a swig from the bottle of South African cooking sherry she's found, and passes it to me, planting a sherry-flavoured kiss on my cheek as she does so.

As I am always honest with you, I have to admit that this Peeping Tom bit is quite a turn-on.

Did I mention that each time the music stops, the girls left in all have to take off an article of clothing? I didn't? Well, they do, and there is soon a pile of boots, tights, blouses and jumpers and one or two other things, growing in the corner by the sofa.

And the growing number of couples dancing lying-down all over the place.

And a growing Edgar in my strides.

'I think I'm losing control, Jonny,' hisses Seraphina.

'Well, you won't find it stuck down the front of my trousers,' I hiss back, finding that my right arm has somehow slipped down inside the lady's blouse, and is caressing her bra-filler.

'Musical Chairs' is nearing a climax, and it is not the only one. It's amazing how the most unlikely ladies turn out to be turn-on experts. Mrs. Blanco is no great shakes as a looker, though she is a happy looker, yet Edgar knows that he is safely in the hands of a real expert.

There is just enough of Jonny's self-control left to stagger from the kitchen floor, hastily readjusting my dress before leaving, and cram several plates of sausage rolls on a tray, interrupting something in the living-room that is getting to look like an illustrated article in one of the less pleasant Sunday papers.

They break off what they're doing, and I try to close my eyes to what they're doing, while they scoff the whole trayful in about eight seconds.

I make my excuses and leave.

Children of today are dead spoilt. I remember when my old man used to let us have some sweets. But they had to last. Have you ever tried to make one fifth of a jelly baby a week last? And he never even got the boy jelly babies so we'd have had that little bit more.

Back in the kitchen, I am grappled and thrown to the floor by Seraphina.

'Take me. Take me, I'm yours!'

I risk a last glance through the hatch, before surrendering to Mrs. Blanco. Well, it's not polite to refuse a lady. Specially not when she's got her fingers and teeth well entangled in your shorts *and* your curlies.

'Postman's Knock' is just beginning. And already clothes are being taken off. I give up. I've tried. Honest I have. But when that sort of thing is inevitable, then I might as well lie back and enjoy it.

For the several hundredth time in my life I curse the man who invented tights, as we wriggle and roll our way across the floor as I try to get them off Seraphina, while she is determined to keep hold of Edgar.

She can't seem to make her mind up. 'Yes. Oh, yes, Jonny.

Please.' Followed by: 'No. Jonny, if my husband ever finds out about this. No. Yes. Don't. Please. Do.'

In between all this confusing converse, Edgar manages to slide into the torrid tunnel, finding it very much to his tastes. I have no time to taste it, as Seraphina is not a great one for any foreplay. We hardly even get to one-play before she's got her mouth open with a grade-A scream on the way out.

Luckily there is an odd-sausage-roll on the edge of the table and I manage to reach up and cram it in her mouth at the last moment. Phew. Thanks to Walls for stopping the wailing.

After that hurried first gallop, we manage to canter through the next race in a more leisurely fashion. The living-room is totally silent by now, but frankly I am past caring. If that's what they want to do, then let them get on with it, says I. If you can't be good, and why should you? – then at least be careful.

Seraphina is still pressing me (!) and Edgar is eager for more, but time is passing. Charity will soon be back, and there will be mums and dads coming to collect their offsprings. I don't want mums and dads catching them (and me) playing at mums and dads.

So I give Mrs. Blanco a farewell kiss, parting her crocus petals, and help her into her tights again. There is a minor worry when we can't find her knickers, but we finally locate them dangling off the framed calendar of 'Unusual Views', and a very unusual view they make, obscuring the Old Forge at Cowpatte Magna.

She has reassured me that she takes the necessary precautions, so we have a final standing-up quickie with clear consciences. Apart from Lobelia, and Mr. Blanco, ever finding out.

Thinking about precautions reminds me about something Uncle Nick once tells me. He says that the best form of contraceptive is a marble in the right shoe. Because it makes you limp all day.

I haven't forgotten about the fishmonger joke at the end of the chapter. Don't worry, dear.

At last I get rid of all the parents, including Seraphina who has sobered up by now, and they take their children off with them and all is well. Bobby and Faith are both going to the pictures for a special birthday treat. There's a double bill on at the local flea-pit, just for children.

A Womb with a View on with *Ram it in Harder*. The local Young Wives' group went on Monday, and they reckon it's great. But their usual idea of fun is tying ribbons round the pork prodder of some elderly male stripper, so I wouldn't place too much weight on it. Their judgement, not the gift-wrapped goolies!

I sit down and relax, sampling the half-bottle of Polish vodka I have found in the local supermarket. If it touches your teeth it strips the enamel off like a dose of salts, but it does wonders for tiredness.

When I remember something.

Or, rather, I trip over something.

A large holdall, marked with the words: 'Uncle Rupert – Prestigious Prestiditator'. He's been watching *The Good Old Days*.

Uncle Rupert? I quite forgot him. Must still be sleeping it off in the shed while I was having it off in the kitchen. I rush out in the garden, noticing that others have been here before me. It looks as though the children must all have crept quietly out while I was . . . busy, and peeked in to look at Uncle Rupert. There are the marks of several not so tiny feet in the borders. And the padlock is in place outside the door!

From inside I hear muffled groans!

I fumble with the key. Oh, padlocks! There.

Now I see why Bobby and Faith kept sniggering about what a success the entertainer had been. And how they hoped he enjoyed *their* trick as much as they'd enjoyed *his*.

Poor Uncle Rupert.

The children have had a lot of fun. There were several cans of paint in the shed, and they have decorated Uncle Rupert with some amazing designs. They obviously had designs on him from the start. There are slogans like: 'Last Heroes Rule. O.K.?' and pictures that are appropriately enough done in blue.

Uncle Angus once had a job in a drawing office, but he packs it in when he finds out that blueprints aren't dirty pictures.

While he was 'resting' the children spread-eagled Uncle Rupert against the wall, and tied his hands and feet out like a cross. And I'd be cross if they'd done it to me. To stop him making a noise, someone stuffed a pair of tights in his mouth, tying the feet behind his neck. The feet of the tights, not Uncle Rupert's!!

I imagine he is not happy, but I can't see his face properly, as someone else, or maybe the same someone, has elegantly draped a pair of peach pink panties over the top of his head.

There is hardly an inch of his body that isn't covered in paint, and someone had found an old pair of spectacle frames and tied them on . . . Well, you know, giving his family jewels a surreal appearance. Teach him to dilly-Dali.

How do I what?

How do I know his body is covered in paint all over it?

Because . . . all together now . . . Rupert, Rupert is bare . . .

It isn't actually a joke about a fishmonger. It's actually a true story about my Uncle Nick who once worked as a fishmonger. With this girl who used to lie on the slab and say fillet.

But that's another tail. Whoops! Got no sole, that's my trouble. Floundering about.

This lady comes into the shop where Uncle Nick is working. Rich bird. All money and no knickers. Know what I mean?

'I say there. My good man.'

After a couple of tries, Uncle Nick realises that the old trout is talking to him.

'Yes, madam. What can I do for you?'

'I would like some cod.'

'Sorry madam,' replies Uncle Nick. 'We have no cod in the shop.'

'Nonsense! Of course you have."

'I'm frightfully sorry, madam. But we don't have any cod at all.'

'Look here, my good man. I have been a customer of this establishment for many years, and you always have cod. Now will you please serve me some cod.'

By now Uncle Nick is getting more than a bit browned off, but he stays polite. 'I hate to disappoint a regular customer, madam, but I have to repeat that there is . . . no . . .cod"

'There must be. Do I have to call the manager?'

'I am the manager,' comes back Uncle N.

'Oh. Then serve me some cod.'

'Madam. What do you get when you take the "P" out of "Plaice"?'

'Lace' replies the puzzled lady.

'Right. And what do you get if you take an "S" out of "Skate"?'

'Kate. But I don't see . . .'

'Finally, madam, what do you get when you take the "F" out of "Cod"?'

Rich lady looks bewildered, and the rest of the shop wait for the punchline.

'But . . . there is no "F" in "Cod".'

'RIGHT!' screams back Uncle Nick triumphantly. 'You got it at last. There's no effin cod!'

Pass further down the book there, please.

CHAPTER TEN

I'm not saying that Charity has a nasty mind, but she's the only person that I know who's stuck bits of razor blade round the edge of her frisbee.

In five days, Lobelia will be back, and I can leave and look for some more openings. Not that my life as a housewife has been lacking in openings.

But they say that best things in life are free. I reckon that the best thing in life is being free. I can't carry on being Lobelia's lapdog for any longer, Jonny must move on.

Only five more days to avoid the temptation of Charity's knickers and the dreadful threat of the blunt scissors. And that's no joke.

Talking of which, I suppose I ought to tell you a bit more about the competition before this adventure races to its climax. If that's the right word.

What you have to do is this. Send in to me, c/o Sphere Books, 30–32 Gray's Inn Road, London, W.C.1, as many jokes as you like. They can be dirty, though very dirty ones won't win the prize. But send them in if you like. Don't send in any racial jokes, because I don't like them at all, and I'm one of the judges!

Closing date for this one will be Easter 1977. After that, it's too late. And don't send in any jokes you've read in my books. I'll recognise them. I'm not saying that ladies who send in naughty pictures and frillies will necessarily have an advantage . . . Not really, but don't let that deter you.

If possible, everyone who sends in a joke or jokes will get a mention in a later episode of my adventure. And the winner will get *ten pounds* and a special mention in a book. So don't forget to put your name and address neatly somewhere so I know who my friends are.

Back to Withering Bumple.

The highlight of these last few days is a visit from a lady of the Press. And the moment I open the door of eighty-four Copper Bottom, I spot that she is a lady that I would not mind pressing.

Five feet ten, if she's an inch. Leather coat with a brown fur collar. Lovely pair of . . . boots on. Fooled you there! And all filled out with a great figure. Living doll, that's what she is. There's a case under her arm, and I reckon she must be some kind of researcher, finding out what telly programmes I watch and what papers I read.

'I only watch *Panorama* and I read the *Times*,' I say, getting, it in quickly. Once you've got it in quickly, then it's a bit late for them to say 'No'.

"No."

Win a few – lose a few.

'I'm a reporter. And you must be Jonathan May?'

Fame at last! !

After all these years, someone somewhere wants to talk to me. Interview me. Must be for Harty Welcome, or whatever his name is. Or Michael Parkinsons-Law. One of that lot. Jolly Jack Frost and his super show.

I'll be a star, a superstar, with a shiny suit and a big . . .

'You are Mister May?'

'Yes. Yes, I am.'

'My name is Vivienne.'

'Vivienne what?'

"Like it?'

'I love it, but what's your name?'

'That is my name. Vivienne Lykitt. Can we go inside, Jonny? Bloody cold out here.'

She is right. I can hear the distant clang of a passing brass monkey. We step inside eighty-four, and she sits down in the deep armchair, revealing more leg than a pole-vaulting giraffe. I lay her over the back of . . . There I go again. I lay her coat over the back of the sofa and go out to make her a coffee.

'All white?' I call in from the kitchen, where I am brewing up the boiling water in a casserole. Must buy another kettle before Lobelia gets back.

'Fine thanks. Are you all right?'

'No.'

'I'm sorry to hear that.'

'I mean I'm all right, but do you want your coffee all white?'

She laughs. 'No. Black please, and no sugar.'

The kitchen is some distance from the living-room, so I nip in and put on a John Stewart album – *California Bloodlines*, beautiful – and finish making the drink.

'I expect you're wondering why I'm here, Jonny?'

I simper prettily.

'Have you got stomach-ache?' asks the reporter lady.

I stop simpering.

'I've heard about you running this house all on your own, with three young children to look after. You see, I write for *Extra Pelvis*, the magazine of the liberated female,' I groan inwardly at this news, but I remember Miss Penny Spender the liberated window-cleaner and my spirits rise. 'And we're specially interested in what you think of role-inversion.'

Role-inversion? Sounds to me like turning a small bun upside-down.

But she is going on.

'But, I must admit that I have another reason for being here today. Does the name of Penny Spender mean anything at all to you?'

What a small world it is! Specially when you're trying to get in a phone booth with three fat ladies, but that's another story.

'Yes. She's the lady who cleans my windows.'

Miss Lykitt smiles. No, she actually grins. Or even leers. 'I know a bit more than that, Jonny. I'm told that she also helps to remove blockages.'

Since Penny has clearly revealed all, I don't feel bound by my usual code of conduct. Better than a code in the nose.

'Actually, Miss Lykitt, I would have said that it was me who was doing the blocking and unblocking.'

'Precisely. You see we liberated women feel that men like you should be castrated.'

By You and Nuck!! What is this preoccupation with blunt scissors that so many women seem to be getting these days? Too much of this and there will be a sharp fall in the birth-rate. And I do mean sharp.

'You go around like you're God's gift to all women, and expect them to fall into your arms and be grateful that you've serviced them. You're just like a prize stallion, Jonny. All **** and no brains.'

If you know what the **** means, then it won't bother you. If you don't, then . . . it won't bother you either.

This is too much. Maybe there are men like she describes, but Jonny has never been one of them. Perhaps I shall simply tell her to sling her hook. Or burn her bra, or something like that.

Unless, there is another way that I can . . .

'However, that's just the way animals like you are made, and it's up to us to help to stamp you out so that later generations will have a better life.'

My hackles are up. No, dear! Hackles. It means I'm getting angry.

'And what are you actually going to do about it, yourself like? And where do I come in?'

'You come in me. Eventually.'

I shake my head, while Edgar nods his. Have I misunderstood Miss Lykitt? Or should that be *Ms* Lykitt? Pronounced Mizz, as in a mizz is as good as a mile.

'You've come here to interview me about running the house.'

'Quite right, Jonny. But I'm also doing a bit for *Extra Pelvis* on what it's like to be the victim of a seduction by a male chauvinist pig. So shall we go upstairs and get on with it? We can take the coffee up with us. And let's get a move on, if that's possible. I want to be back in London before tea-time.'

She gets up, flashing her legs at me, and walks towards the hall door, waiting for me to follow. There is no doubt that Vivienne is a very attractive lady, and one that normally I would get through like a hot spoon through Tasteefreeze.

I stand there in the hall, watching the nicest bottom this side of Twiggy shimmy up the stairs towards the Dugfondle bedroom, and I decide that I have a choice. Mizz Lykitt, like it or not, wants me to give her a dose of the famous May medicine, which involves shaking the bottle before, during and after. In fact, she actually expects me to shoot an arrow or two into her desirable target.

But should I?

I know I want to, but that's not the point. Seems to me that I can either take it or leave it. If I leave it, then she'll be very choked off and that'll be definitely one up to me over the liberated lady.

You know Norman Mailer, the American writer? Wrote *The Naked and the Dead*, and lots of other good books? I don't mean do you know him personally, but you've heard of him? He can't stand fem-lib types either. A year or so back he gets an invite to lecture to a mass of them. Stands up at the beginning of the talk and says: 'I know that you don't like me or what I represent. So get it out in the open. For the next three minutes you can all heckle and boo and hiss me.' They do. Really let it all hang out against him. He holds his hands up after the three minutes have passed, and they all fall silent.

Mailer looks them over and grins. 'Obedient set of bitches, aren't you?' he says.

Now I can let her lie up there for a bit and then throw her out on her donkey. Or is the word 'ass'?

Or I can give her the best going-over and coming-under she's ever had. Or, since she doesn't seem enthusiastic, the best she's never had.

What a choice. The only way I can fail is if I try her and can't make it. That would be one down to me!

I'll give you five seconds to decide which I do. The safe way and chuck her out, or take the risk and give her what she wants only more so. Which do you think?

Five seconds.

Four.

Three.

Two.

One.

Time's up.

I think I'll come back next week, Nicholas, and try for the kitchen and the freezer and the meat and the fish and the cakes and the tarts. But most of all the tarts.

If you noticed that the page was going a bit wobbly, that's because we are now having a flash forward. Which is what my Uncle Nick is always getting arrested for. Mainly little girls coming home after hockey. Aunt Holly sometimes goes to court as a character witness, but he finally stops her. After she tells the judge that Uncle Nick spends three quarters of his married life thinking about sex and the other quarter having it.

We are now half an hour before tea-time.

The scene is the bedroom, children. That's because they should be scene and not heard.

'Jonny?'

'What?'

'Do it again to me.'

'Ask properly.'

'Please, Jonny. Pretty please, do it again to little Vivienne.'

'Do what?' I can be tough when I have to. Well, it's better to be cruel to be kind.

'You know. That bit where you nibble me here, while your fingers stroke me, there. Then you put *that* in here, while you lick me here. And here. Then, when I can't stand it any longer, you stop touching me here and here, and put *that* in here, while your right hand goes here, and rubs this, and your other hand goes right up there.'

I bet you readers wish this was illustrated. If it was we could all meet up in the courtroom.

So I do everything Viv wants, and get the same effect as the other eight times I have already done it.

(Publisher's Note: Eight?)

Yes. I sometimes think I've had enough after eight. He reckons he's on top of the world at one. They call him William Softcastle.

Some of you ladies will be a little incensed, not to mention the gold and myrrh, at the ease with which I have seduced this strong-willed lady, and will think what a male chauvinist pig I really am.

Come on now, girls. She actually asked me for it. And when I give it her, it's all a bit more than she reckons on. The first time wasn't easy, with her lying there like a dead polar bear, and me working away like a docker on overtime.

But after number three, she starts to relax more. Gets those soft thighs spread a little wider. Sticks the 'Welcome' sign on the gates. And I do come well.

By number five Mizz is more like a Miss, though a hit with me. And is taking the initiative. In both hands. Edgar enjoys the exercise, taking his afternoon dip in the warm pool.

Afterwards, she lets me untie her – whoops, what a give-away! – and kisses me hard on the lips. Lets me help her get dressed, giggling as I have a spot of trouble pulling up her panties. They seem to get entangled in me, or I in them, and this leads to a further delay in her leaving.

I watch her walk, a trifle unsteadily, down Copper Bottom, turning at the bend to wave goodbye and blow me a kiss. My lips are so sore that I have a job to blow one back. Never like those blow jobs anyway. No substitute for the real thing, are they?

Last I hear, Miss Lykitt has resigned from *Extra Pelvis* and got a job working as a Penthouse Pet.

I reckon she's happier as well. And I'm *not* a chauvinist pig. Not, not, *not*. Cross my heart and hope to oink. Oink, Oink, Oink! ! !

CHAPTER ELEVEN

My Uncle Angus once had a nasty experience while driving in the country. Roaring along in his Morris Minor at thirty-five. Well, he has a following wind. When he goes round a corner, and there's this big black bull. Screeching of brakes, but Uncle Angus has no chance, hits the bull, and kills it stone dead.

Very worried he is, and so he goes up the nearby farmhouse, and knocks. Farmer opens it and asks him what he wants.

'I'm dreadfully sorry,' says Uncle A., 'but I've just run over a big black bull.'

'Dang me!' exclaims the farmer, spitting out a mouthful of straw. 'He were my best old boy, that 'un.'

'Very sorry,' says Uncle Angus. 'But I'll do anything that I can to replace him.'

'Does 'ee mean that?' asks the farmer.

'Of course. Anything at all.'

'Right then. There's eighteen cows in that barn there. You'll find a hook behind the door to hang your trousers on.'

Lobelia is due back today. Her card says her flight gets her in at two and she should be sailing up Copper Bottom about four. As she comes in, so I shall drift out, my job done, ready to find a new challenge for the May wits.

(Publisher's Note: He needs only half a challenge, as he's a half-wit.)

If you want to read the collected humour of my publisher, it's on display in the third cubicle, Gent's toilet, Charing Cross Road.

Charity and I decide to have a last drink together to celebrate. Bobby and Faith have gone off to some friends, but have promised to be back in time to greet their mother. Bobby has said that he hopes they'll be able to give her a nice surprise to greet her. I don't know what it is. Probably a fretwork lampshade or something like that.

Their friend has a new pet monkey, who they claim likes cakes. I suppose it must be a meringue-outang.

As I look back on the last six weeks, I am surprised how well they have gone. The twins have forgiven my angry outburst at the beginning, and haven't come up with any nasty revenge, like I reckoned they might.

And I have kept out of Charity's knickers. And thus away from the blunt scissors.

Only another couple of hours.

Nothing can go wrong now.

'Oh, Jonny.'

'Oh, Charity.'

I'm afraid so. You see, my lord, it was like this. There's this bottle of what I think is ordinary vodka, and Charity urges me to have a couple of snorts for old times' sake. To celebrate the end of our happy time together.

What she doesn't tell me is that the vodka is very unordinary, being something like one hundred and forty proof. About double the normal stuff. And the proof of the vodka is in the pudding-like feel my brain assumes.

After three, or is it four, of them? Charity comes and sits on my lap in the spare room, where we have somehow found ourselves. There is one of those beds that springs down from the wall, and we are sitting on that. Nothing is further from my mind than blunt scissors.

'You do like me, don't you, Jonny?' asks Charity, letting her young fingers toy with my little dinky Edgar. I just love these dinky toys.

As Edgar is doing his best to impersonate Nelson's Column, it would be silly of me to pretend that I don't fancy her. My finger biscuits are crunching their way through Charity's undergrowth, probing in among the family hairloom. The famous knickers that we have seen and heard so much about are still in their place, and what a pretty place it is, too! But I have found an interesting detour, that takes my hand a' wandering up a side entrance, into the fairy grotto, where the walls are already becoming moist and warm.

The fold-down bed is a useful thing to have around the house, and I am glad that I have been round and tidied up everything, getting in new pots, pans, plates and cutlery, as well as changing all the bedclothes.

I can hear the radio on in the other room, that seems to be stuck halfway between channels. I can hear Joan Bakewell talking about wallpaper, and also a commentary on the Derby County match against Wolves. What with Derby and Joan, I can't concentrate, so I get up, with some difficulty owing to an obstruction in the lower fly, and turn it off.

Charity quickly pulls me back on the bed, and finds that I am not turned off. Next thing I know is that we are both under the bedclothes, and neither of us have any bed clothes on. Or any other sort of clothes. Charity's knickers have come off in my hand, as has Charity herself. Things are beginning to get hazy, and there are gaps in my memory. But I still remember that someone or other told me to make sure that Charity takes off her panties in bed, and I've certainly done that.

Indeed, I have gone one better. I have taken steps (but I'll put them back later) to make sure that while I'm around, it's not going to be possible for her to get them back on again. Not with Edgar guarding the doorway, and sticking his head in and out to make sure all is well.

All is very well indeed.

Except that someone has turned the lights out!

And I know that this naughtiness can lead to feeling the earth move, and all that, but I've never actually known it to throw you right upside-down while you were still getting stuck in!

Is it sweet Charity and her charms?

Or is it the vodka?

Here is a suspense break. Like a coffee break, only for suspenders. Keep you guessing as I near the climax.

Of the book.

Actually, not only of the book.

What can have happened to make Jonny imagine that the bed and him and her in it has suddenly tipped the wrong way up?

Would you believe that it's because the bed and him and her in it has been tipped the wrong way up?

No.

Yes.

Someone, and I would not bet a Richard Nixon campaign button on it not being a certain heavenly pair of twins, has pulled the knob (! ?) that releases the bed, and sends it swinging back into the wall.

So, here I am, immovably locked into Charity, nearly suffocating, with her mother due home any moment. How will Jonny wriggle free from this one? I hear you asking.

He won't, I reply.

And he doesn't.

Charity does succeed in getting free of Edgar, but the space between the bed and the wall is so small that even a dwarf snail would be uncomfortable. And all she can do is wriggle around to try and get in a less incriminating position.

She doesn't exactly manage it.

Edgar may have lost his grip on pussy power, but her contortions result in her being the other way up, so that her face is somewhere round about the lower part of my stomach. Notice how tactfully I put it. This also means that my face is firmly buried between her thighs, which I ought to remind you are still knickerless.

Every time I try and open my mouth to call for help, she starts giggling and biting her teeth dangerously close to Edgar.

When I get up this morning, the sun is shining, and I think that it looks as though it would be a perfect day for running into Twiggy.

Slowly.

But things are not turning out well. I feel sure that Faith and Bobby are at the bottom of this, but I am too busily involved with Charity's bottom to do anything about it.

If this goes on any longer, then Lobelia will be home, and I can't imagine her being happy with what she finds. I can just imagine her: 'What do you think you're doing?'

Aah. At last. Through all the layers of bed and blankets, not to mention bed and bawd, I hear a hand clicking the catch to let the bed down again. What a let-down.

'What do you think you're doing?'

At least I guessed right. But the printed word can't hope to convey the depth of anger in Lobelia's voice. I struggle to my feet, reaching automatically for my trousers, as I suss that a fast exit is going to be needed. A bronzed Lobelia has run screaming for the kitchen, while her knickerless daughter, and the greatest of them all *is* Charity, runs after her. I can hear the late love of my life rummaging through the cutlery drawer, shouting out something scissors. Blunt scissors, could it be?

Faith and Bobby are grinning at me round the corner of the door, as I tug on a shirt, and topple over trying for my socks. Both legs at once. Well, I am not about to stick around for the unkindest cut of all. And after I kept her house going for her for six weeks. Anyone would think I'd make a muck-up of it. And ended up with seducing her daughter into the . . . but we'll let that pass.

In my hurry, I fail to notice this beaming black man sitting bewilderedly in a chair, looking at me.

'Who are you?' I ask, zipping up my boots.

'I am Idi,' he replies in something approximating to English. 'I now boy for Lobelia and am in for good time. In my house.'

'Your house?'

'Yes, I Idi am in my house.'

'You're welcome to it, Idi,' shout I. I mean, me. As I button up my shirt. That's me dressed at last. There's the door.

And here comes Lobelia, waving the often-mentioned pair of serrated snippers in her hand, mouth open like a stand-in from 'Jaws'.

Time, my friends to bid farewell to the work of women, which is never done, anyway. And take the usual long steps towards fresh fields and pastures new. Don't think it hasn't been fun, because it hasn't. But there've been a few laughs, and even a fair bit of the ups and downs.

Next time I'll take on something more restful. Like taming tarantulas, or swallowing goldfish.

I slam the door in Lobelia's face, and bid a very rapid good-bye to Mrs. Vatman as she leans out of her upstairs window.

Eighty-four Copper Bottom is soon a blur in the distance. Fortunately, there is a train at Withering Bumple station, and I am soon on board it, heading for London and a bit of peace and quiet.

Maybe Liz James will be back in town again.

Something will turn up for Jonny. It always does.

Doesn't it?

Don't forget the jokes and things.

And here's a last quickie for you. Do you know what happens

to people who can't tell the difference between vaseline and putty?

All their windows fall out.

Byeeeee!

Das Buch

August 1914: Der Kriegsausbruch macht dem russischen Sozialisten Wladimir Iljitsch Uljanow, der sich Lenin nennt, einen Strich durch seine Rechnung. Statt, wie beabsichtigt, von einem Dorf im österreichischen Galizien aus die Proletarier aller Länder zu mobilisieren, muß er sich in ein neutrales Land absetzen. 1916 trifft er in Zürich ein. Doch hier sind seine revolutionären Ideen nicht zu verwirklichen, und er zieht sich resigniert in Bibliothekssäle zurück, unentschieden, ob er nach Amerika auswandern oder in seine Heimat zurückkehren soll. Wir wissen, wie er sich entschieden hat: Im April 1917 durchquert er mit Unterstützung der deutschen Militärs in einem verplombten Reichsbahnwaggon Deutschland in Richtung St. Petersburg. Die Stadt wird wenig später Leningrad heißen.
«Solschenizyn will mit diesem historisch-psychologischen Porträt aus Dokument und Deutung einen entscheidenden Moment der Weltgeschichte erhellen, Ereignisse, die den Gang der Geschichte bestimmt haben, aber dem Blick der Historiker sorgsam verborgen blieben» (François Bondy in «Die Weltwoche»). Ursprünglich als ein Kapitel in «August Vierzehn» vorgesehen, sah sich Solschenizyn durch seine eigene Emigration in die Schweiz und das dadurch ermöglichte Quellenstudium dazu veranlaßt, Lenins Schweizer Aufenthalt zu einem selbständigen Buch auszuarbeiten.

Der Autor

Alexander Solschenizyn wurde am 11. Dezember 1918 in Kislowodsk geboren. Er war Mathematiklehrer und im Zweiten Weltkrieg Offizier. Nach Kriegsende verhaftet, in Straflagern interniert und dann nach Mittelasien verbannt, wurde er erst 1956/57 rehabilitiert. Nach heftigen Angriffen wurde er 1969 aus dem sowjetischen Schriftstellerverband ausgeschlossen und 1974, als «Archipel GULAG» im Westen erschien, aus der Sowjetunion ausgewiesen. Er lebte erst in Zürich und seit 1976 in den USA. 1970 Nobelpreis für Literatur. Auf deutsch liegen u. a. vor: «Der Archipel GULAG», «August Vierzehn», «Der erste Kreis der Hölle», «Krebsstation» und Erzählungen.